THE FORBIDDEN HOUSE

LA MAISON INTERDITE

THE FORBIDDEN HOUSE

Michel Herbert & Eugène Wyl

Translated by John Pugmire

First published in French in 1932 by
Librarie Gallimard as *La Maison interdite*
Copyright © Librarie Gallimard
THE FORBIDDEN HOUSE
English translation copyright © by John Pugmire 2021.

Every effort has been made to trace the holders of copyright. In the event of any inadvertent transgression of copyright, the editor would like to hear from the authors' representatives. Please contact me at pugmire1@ yahoo.com.

Cover design by Joseph Gérard

FIRST AMERICAN EDITION
Library of Congress Cataloguing-in-Publication Data
Herbert, Michel & Wyl, Eugène
[*La Maison interdite* English]
The Forbidden House /Michel Herbert & Eugène Wyl
Translated from the French by John Pugmire

INTRODUCTION

Very little is known about the authors, Michel Herbert and Eugène Wyl, except that the former was active in revolutionary politics as a journalist, pamphleteer, and songwriter, and the latter's real name was Eugène Lejarre. Together, they wrote three impossible crime novels in the 1930s, of varying quality.

This first, *The Forbidden House* (La Maison interdite, 1932) is rated ***** (Chef d'oeuvre) in Roland Lacourbe's admirable *1001 Chambres Closes,* which describes the denouement as "a triumph of Cartesian logic."

The central puzzle is one of the most baffling in impossible crime fiction: a mysterious stranger, whose face cannot be seen by the several witnesses outside the house, is introduced inside, where he murders the owner and vanishes without trace. The several witnesses inside cannot explain what happened. A search of the house fails to find him, and the witnesses watching the outside say he could not have left.

The authorities—examining magistrate, state prosecution, and police—trying to make sense of the clues, cannot agree amongst themselves as to the identity of the murderer...

An interesting feature of the book is a detailed re-enactment of a typical French (and Continental European) trial, which differs markedly from the process in force in the Anglosphere. Appendix I explains the differences between the judicial systems.

John Pugmire
New York

FIRST PART

A MAN ENTERED

I

A powerful, silent, shiny luxury limousine stopped, after skilfully negotiating a bend, in front of the steps of Marchenoire Manor.

The guard, deferential and attentive, ran down to open the rear door and withdrew.

A portly individual with a face like a round scarlet ball perched on a low collar, and a corpulent body clad in a mauve suit, placed a foot compressed into a canary-yellow shoe tentatively on the ground and got out.

With his short fingers, each adorned with sparkling rings, the new arrival fished a monocle with a tortoiseshell frame out of his fob watch pocket and fixed it in his left eye.

He contemplated with intense satisfaction the part of the park which extended in front of the manor: a vast lawn bisected by a central drive covered with a layer of pink gravel, in the middle of which glistened the stagnant water of a defunct circular fountain.

He turned to look at the building, three storeys high and covered with heavy statues and pretentious ornaments.

A semi-circular protuberance attracted the fat man's attention:

'Now that's a real manor,' he exclaimed. 'It's got a turret!'

A frail, pale, effeminate adolescent with a refined elegance got out of the vehicle and minced towards him.

The other greeted him joyfully:

'Ah, Marquis... I'm delighted!... This residence is superb! What distinction! What style!'

The Adonis retorted with a smile:

'Third Republic style, guaranteed authentic.'

The portly individual did not notice the irony.

'Ah!' he replied simply, 'it's possible. You know this sort of thing better than I.'

Two more individuals got out of the limousine: both of them cold, solemn, thin, precise, tight-lipped, smooth, and dressed in black.

One of them was old, round-shouldered, and unctuous. He stroked his long white beard with gloved hands. The other was a timid-looking young man with a clean-shaven, pockmarked face; he was awkwardly carrying a briefcase stuffed with papers.

The older man asked, slowly and self-importantly:

'And what did I tell you, Monsieur Verdinage?... Was I wrong to advise you to purchase this magnificent property?... A splendid manor of approximately two hundred square metres, with all modern comforts, telephone, electricity, plus a small guardhouse, all in a park of five hectares, entirely walled, situated right in the forest of l'Aigle, close to Compiègne, on an incomparable site! ... And all of it being given away at a ridiculous price!... You can buy it for next to nothing!'

The fat man shrugged his shoulders as he replied:

'The price isn't important, Maître Laridoire (1). What counts is that I like it. You can sort out the details of the sale with the Marquis Adhémar Dupont-Lesguyères, my secretary.'

The instruction was issued with an air of indifference as he indicated the elegant Adonis who was following him.

'Very well,' replied Me. Laridoire, 'but before that, Monsieur Verdinage, would you allow me to show you the building?... The interior is worthy of the exterior... I don't think you'll be disappointed.'

At a sign from the old man, the guard approached.

He was a solid peasant, about thirty years old. An invasive moustache covered much of his face. Little blinking eyes, wily and cunning, peeped out from under bushy eyebrows, giving him a rather untrustworthy appearance.

He moved with his body inclined forward, in a servile attitude.

'Allow me to introduce Bénard, Jacques Bénard, the vigilant watchdog of the property,' continued Me. Laridoire. 'Bénard has been here for five years, in other words, since the construction of the manor. He has never ceased the maintenance and surveillance of the property, even when Marchenoire was unoccupied.'

---

(1) an honorific for lawyers, abbreviated to Me.

'It's true, monsieur,' muttered the guard, twisting his thick woollen cap around in his fingers. 'It's true! I'm almost a fixture.'

Me. Laridoire turned towards Verdinage:

'I'm happy to recommend Bénard,' he said. 'If you purchase Marchenoire, as you intend to do, you won't find a better guardian than this humble servant.'

'Monsieur is going to buy the...?' asked Bénard, astonishment showing on his face.

He stopped himself and, after an embarrassed silence, turned to the would-be future owner and declared, in an unctuous tone:

'I hope monsieur would like to employ me. I know the park like the back of my hand.'

'We'll see about that,' replied Verdinage curtly.

The offhand response appeared to disappoint the guard, who was obviously hoping for a warmer welcome.

At that moment a cripple emerged, limping, from the left angle of the manor, circumnavigated the turret and stopped in surprise at the sight of the group at the front entrance.

The guard directed his bad mood at the new arrival, marching towards him shouting:

'Go away, Clodoche! Get out of here! And quickly!'

The man limped away, and the guard turned back to Verdinage:

'It's Clodoche,' he explained, 'a poor cripple that I've taken under my wing out of charity. Nobody else wanted him. He's not quite right in the head, but he helps me as best he can. There's enough work for two in a property the size of Marchenoire.'

'Stop bullying that poor man,' ordered the lawyer, 'and show us around inside.'

Bénard opened the door of the manor, using a key he pulled out of one of the pockets of his military jacket.

Standing in the entrance hall, the fat man exclaimed enthusiastically:

'Perfect!... Magnificent!... The architect didn't skimp on the marble....'

'Nor the gold leaf!' gushed Adhémar Dupont-Lesguyères.

'Look at the garlands of roses, the lyres, the ornamental mouldings,' added Verdinage. 'It looks rich!'

'And even *nouveau-riche*!'

Verdinage recoiled at the overly direct pleasantry. He looked anxiously at his impassive secretary.

Without adding a word, he went into the first room to the right.

'We're in the library,' explained the lawyer. 'There must be ten-thousand books here!'

The fat man instructed the secretary:

'Marquis, buy enough volumes to make sure the shelves are all filled. Choose the best books in each genre.'

'Very well, monsieur. Which authors do you prefer?'

'I couldn't care less! I just want to decorate the walls of my library. You surely can't imagine that I wish to amuse myself by reading ten-thousand books! I haven't got that much time to waste. I didn't become executive director of a chain of groceries by dilly-dallying, believe me!'

He stopped to look at a monumental fireplace in the middle of one of the walls.

'Good grief, this one's in stone. Couldn't they have built it marble, like all the rest? These architects really have no taste.'

'You don't like the fireplace?' asked Me. Laridoire in astonishment. 'It's a perfect specimen, nevertheless. The first owner of Marchenoire had it imported from a twelfth-century castle, which was demolished shortly afterwards. You can see a plaque bearing the coat of arms of the nobleman at the rear of the hearth.'

Verdinage turned again to his secretary:

'Marquis,' he said, 'make sure that rusty old plaque is replaced with a new one.'

'And we could replace the coat of arms with that of the grocery chain,' suggested Dupont-Lesguyères, keeping a straight face.

'Good idea,' said the fat man. 'I don't see why I should have some unknown fellow's plaque in my own castle.'

The elderly lawyer led him out of the room.

'On the other side of the hall,' he continued, 'we have a series of reception rooms. When the connecting doors are open, the dining room, large salon, and small salon form a magnificent space fourteen metres long and five metres wide. I won't bother to show you the butlery, kitchen, and linen room. And there's one more room next to the library that could be used as a smoking room, an office, or a boudoir, as you see fit. That's all for the ground floor... Now I propose that we visit the upper quarters.'

The visitors had arrived at the end of the hallway.

Me. Laridoire indicated two staircases, one of which descended to the cellars, whilst the other led upstairs.

The guard touched the peak of his cap respectfully.

'Beg pardon, Monsieur Laridoire,' he said. 'Perhaps it's not necessary that I accompany you upstairs?'

'It actually won't be necessary,' confirmed the lawyer. 'You may go, Bénard. Just remember to lock the front door after we've left.'

'Rest assured,' replied the guard. 'The key won't leave my pocket. When you're not here, I defy anyone to gain access without my permission.'

As they visited the rooms on the upper floor, Verdinage designated each of them as if he were already the owner.

'This will be my smoking room; this will be my billiards room; this will be my bathroom. Here's my bedroom, and over there is my secretary's. My housemaid-nanny and my butler will occupy the small room next to my library on the ground floor. That way, she'll have fewer stairs to climb and her husband's service will be made easier.

Becoming more and more expansive, the fat man walked around each room in turn, opened every window to admire the view, banged on each panel with a huge fist to assure himself of its solidity, tried all the switches, and became ecstatic at the sight of the ostentatious chandeliers and wall lights, distributed, if not with taste, at least with extravagance.

Marchenoire Manor was indeed the residence of his dreams.

He turned to speak to the elderly lawyer, a beatific smile on his wide face:

'When my housemaid-nanny cradled me as a baby in rags, she could never have dreamt that one day I would be the owner of Marchenoire!'

He paced back and forth, beaming and satisfied, already in the role of master of the house.

Lord of the manor!... He couldn't believe he was pronouncing the words. He looked back at himself in 1914, a small grocer without ambition, destined for a life of mediocrity. Then came the war, a tragedy for many, a boon for a lucky few.

On the recommendation of a friend, Verdinage had managed to get an order from the government. Other orders had followed, bringing first affluence, then a fortune.

When peace came, he founded a grocers' association, of which he became executive director. Under his direction the enterprise prospered. After years of hard work, Verdinage, now a multi-millionaire, felt it was about time to take some well-earned rest.

The advertisement of a great property for sale had led him to the chambers of Me. Laridoire, a lawyer in Compiègne.

From the time of his first visit, Marchenoire had captivated him with its vast dimensions and its rather vulgar taste.

'There's another floor above,' said the lawyer. 'It contains an attic and two rooms under the eaves.'

'I shall put my valet in one of the rooms, and my chauffeur and my cook in the other,' declared Verdinage. 'That way everyone will be housed on the premises... All we need now is to sign the purchase contract. Me. Laridoire, did your clerk bring the necessary papers?'

'We have all that we need,' replied the other.

The fat man turned to his secretary:

'Marquis, have you checked the contract thoroughly? Is everything in order?'

'Everything is exactly as agreed, monsieur. All it needs is your signature.'

'Very well. In that case, let's go down to my library. We'll be perfectly at ease there to finalise everything.'

Me. Laridoire looked startled and murmured:

'*In the library?*'

'Well, yes,' grunted Verdinage, surprised by the other's curious attitude. 'Do you find that inconvenient?'

'No... that is... if that's your wish,' mumbled the lawyer.

They descended the staircase.

Adhémar Dupont-Lesguyères was the first to enter the library.

He immediately noticed the letter displayed prominently on the mantelpiece of the monumental fireplace.

'Well, well! The postman's been whilst we were upstairs,' joked the Adonis, as he reached out a hand.

The lawyer rushed forward:

'*Don't touch it!*' he said in a choked voice.

But the secretary had already seen the typed address:

TO THE NEW OWNER OF
MARCHENOIRE MANOR
IN COMPIÈGNE (OISE).

'Don't touch it! For the love of God, don't touch it!' repeated Me. Laridoire, attempting to grab hold of the letter.

Intrigued, Verdinage pushed the man aside almost brutally and picked up the letter addressed to him. He unsealed the envelope and pulled out a sheet of onionskin paper on which the following lines had been typed:

MARCHENOIRE, THIS AUGUST 28,
IF YOU WANT TO LIVE, LEAVE MARCHENOIRE MANOR
IMMEDIATELY AND FOREVER. DO NOT PURCHASE THE
FORBIDDIN HOUSE

The fat man looked up.

The lawyer was shaking like a leaf. The little clerk, as white as a sheet, leant against the wall so as not to fall.

Adhémar Dupont-Lesguyères stuttered:

'The forbidden house... The forbidden house....'

Verdinage burst out laughing; underscoring the penultimate word of the demand notice with the bitten nail of his fat thumb, he cried out jovially:

'Well, well! Marquis, you can see that I'm not the only one to make spelling mistakes. My anonymous correspondent spells "forbidden" with an " i!"'

And he added, with a howl of mirth that made the charms on the watch chain dance on his stomach:

'Who's the idiot who's played this stupid joke?'

'You're right... it's a joke... a stupid joke!' stammered Me. Laridoire. 'Needless to say, it doesn't change your intention?'

'Not at all!' the fat man replied. 'I'm buying Marchenoire Manor, and I intend to move in as soon as possible.'

'But, monsieur...,' protested Adhémar feebly.

Verdinage shrugged his shoulders.

'What?... The threat?... Don't you realise it's the work of a prankster?'

He concluded, with a loud guffaw:

'Only a prankster would use a fireplace as a letter box!'

Happy to have made such a facetious remark, the *nouveau-riche* gave the lawyer a friendly slap which made Me. Laridoire's back bend even more.

. . . .

And it was that episode—in which Napoléon Verdinage refused to see anything more than a "prank"—which marked the start of the unfathomable mystery of Marchenoire Manor.

II

Teams of masons, carpenters, lazy plumbers, electricians, painters and wallpaper hangers had taken possession of the building and, under the direction of Adhémar Dupont-Lesguyères, were working actively on a thousand transformations, extensions, and embellishments.

The marquis had immediately fallen out of favour with the workers under his command, and even with the villagers of Marchenoire, due to his haughty and disdainful attitude. As of the second day, the guard refused to accept his authority.

The two men seemed on the point of coming to blows, but, faced with Bénard's muscular build, the feeble Adonis beat a hasty retreat. He made a show of muttering vague threats as he turned his back on his adversary.

There were two places in the village of Marchenoire where the locals congregated: the wash house, reserved for the women, and the main room of the café *Ménard jeune*, reserved for the men.

In the wash house, as in the café, the gossip was endless. The more malicious gossips, always the best informed, told how Adhémar Dupont-Lesguyères, after a troubled adolescence, ended up in the service of Napoléon Verdinage.

According to them, the marquis had left home at a very young age. Free and reckless, he gave himself over to debauchery, frequenting dubious establishments and choosing his friends amongst the worst members of the Montmartre underworld.

For an entire year, he sponged off a poor young girl who was seduced by the noble title and rascally charm of the young delinquent. One day she was killed in a brawl.

Deprived of his means of support and forced to sustain himself by other means, Adhémar wrote a cheque that bounced. A complaint was lodged and then withdrawn, due to the intervention of the Dupont-Lesguyères family. Having escaped prison by the skin of his teeth, the culprit promised to reform.

Verdinage was looking for a secretary.

Adhémar was interviewed and offered the job.

His natural air of distinction quickly impressed the fat man, who had remained vulgar despite his millions.

The grocer took pride in having an authentic aristocrat in his service. He relied on him for advice on dress conventions and social behaviour. Dupont-Lesguyères became, to all intents and purposes, Verdinage's head of protocol.

Which is why the fat man left the conversion of the manor to the taste and initiative of his secretary.

. . . .

When everything was finally ready, Verdinage arrived with his personal staff, which comprised, in addition to Adhémar Dupont-Lesguyères, a butler, a valet, a chauffeur, a cook, and a housekeeper.

The grocer, normally strict towards his servants, was extremely indulgent towards his butler and housekeeper, Charles and Thérèse Chapon.

Thérèse Chapon had once been the nanny of the new owner, who—with a touching but rather ridiculous tenderness—continued to address her as "Housemaid-nanny."

She resignedly accepted that mode of address and felt compelled, out of reciprocity, to address him as "little one," or "Napo."

Despite the seventy years which had rendered his hair and sideburns white, Charles, Thérèse's husband, attempted valiantly to discharge his responsibilities. He was, unfortunately, hampered in his endeavours by his devotion to the bottle. Under the influence of drink, the butler became forgetful and maladroit. For some time now, the deterioration in his performance had become noticeable.

On several occasions, Verdinage had deemed it necessary to chastise the old servant, who had solemnly vowed each time to change his ways. But, each time, the butler forgot his drunken pledge and returned to his old habits.

In deference to their age, the grocer had decided to lodge them in the ground floor room adjacent to the library, from whence Charles could easily keep an eye on the kitchen and the cellar.

The personnel of Marchenoire Manor included another husband-and-wife team, composed of the chauffeur and the cook. Edmond and Jeanne Tasseau, although no longer a young married couple, still lived in the ecstasy of their honeymoon. Their principal occupation consisted—during those hours when they were not performing their duties—of looking into each other's eyes and smiling beatifically.

As for the valet, Gustave Colinet, who performed his duties with zeal and efficiency, he sought solitude and stayed shut in his room during his leisure hours.

The misanthropy of this young man of twenty years had surprised the other servants at first.

Thérèse Chapon—who saw herself as a bit of a psychologist—declared at once that "It's not normal", then, after lengthy reflection, announced that "there must be a woman behind it."

Verdinage enjoyed being amongst his numerous servants, to whom had been added, since he began residence at Marchenoire, the guard-gardener Bénard and his henchman Clodoche.

The grocer, a decent man, happy and satisfied, had the instinctive compassion that those with good health and good fortune have for the weakness and misery of the underdogs.

Clodoche had, as the result of a complicated fracture of the pelvis, a pronounced limp which caused him to drag a half-paralysed leg behind him as he advanced by leaning heavily on a crutch. As a consequence, one shoulder was higher than the other and his head leant to one side.

This deformity obliged him to pivot awkwardly on his crutch whenever he turned to face his questioner.

A shock of red hair, untouched by any comb, surmounted a broad face with a narrow forehead. The eyes, red and puffy, blinked continually, as if affected by the light, and watered incessantly.

Whenever he encountered the unfortunate fellow during his wanderings around the park, the proprietor made a point of uttering words of encouragement.

At the sight of the cripple, Verdinage became his true self again: he could forget worldly constraints and employ a few slang words without risking an ironic observation from Adhémar Dupont-Lesguyères or watching a reproachful pout appear on the lips of the elegant secretary.

Furthermore, Clodoche, an obliging listener, only responded in monosyllables to the interminable rants of his boss.

For those two reasons the grocer, who had remained a simple man, sought out the company of the cripple.

It was a week since Verdinage had taken up residence in the manor. On that clear September morning he was strolling along the driveway which led to the front gate.

As usual, he called out to Clodoche, who was conscientiously raking the lawns.

'So, my good Clodoche, you're taking care of my grass!'

The cripple swivelled on his crutch and tipped his huge straw hat.

Verdinage was about to continue on his way when he noticed that the fountain halfway down the drive only contained a few inches of stagnant rainwater.

'Clodoche, my friend, I'm going to issue instructions to have this fountain cleaned out and the jet restored to working order.'

The invalid, still leaning on his crutch, looked in astonishment at the owner and laughed stupidly.

Verdinage added:

'There has to be water in the fountain, because without water it's no longer a fountain. Isn't that so, Clodoche?'

Having made that witty remark, the grocer stuck his thumbs in the armholes of his jacket and continued his walk with a satisfied air.

A sudden cry caused him to turn around.

'Napo! Napo! Little one!'

Thérèse Chapon, obviously distressed, arrived out of breath.

'I already told you, Housemaid-Nanny, not to call me that in front of the servants!' said Verdinage angrily. 'I can tolerate those affectionate terms in private, but in public you must set an example of ... of....' Unable to find the right word, he left the sentence unfinished.

'That's exactly what it's about,' sighed the old woman, raising her arms to the sky. 'That's what it's about.'

'What is it? Speak up,' interposed the agitated owner.

'Ah, Nap...Sorry!... Ah, sir. If you only knew what they told me.'

Thérèse Chapon was the only one in the manor who was in daily contact with the villagers.

In order to stock up she made frequent trips to the café *Ménard jeune*, whose landlord—simultaneously innkeeper, grocer, fruit merchant, butcher, baker, and petrol salesman—was the principal shopkeeper of the village.

Whenever she entered the smoke-filled room, her basket on her arm, there was always some peasant there, keen to study the "stranger" from close up.

The peasant would walk around Thérèse, risking some remark about the weather or the high price of condiments, then, once conversation had been engaged, casually enquire as to the wealth, the personal integrity, or the past of the new owner of the estate.

The housekeeper would not reply, and her discretion would draw unflattering remarks from the ladies of the communal wash house and the drinkers at the *Ménard jeune*.

But there would always be one or two who wouldn't give up trying to prise the desired information from Thérèse. The questions would multiply inexorably, demanding ever more precision.

This time it was an old gossip who went by the name of "La Perrette" who decided to tackle her. After looking around to make sure nobody was watching, the old shrew murmured:

'I'm not trying to give you advice... Your boss seems very rich, but perhaps not rich enough to buy himself a real castle... So he had to make do with Marchenoire... He was wrong!... Too bad for him... It was his choice... After all they say about it, it was really tempting the Gods to buy *the forbidden house!*'

The housekeeper trembled as she reported the bad news to Verdinage.

The forbidden house....

The fat man was stunned.

He hastened back to the château, went hurriedly into the library, opened one of the desk drawers, and retrieved a sheet of onion paper.

It was the anonymous letter he had found during his first visit to the property.

He re-read the typed lines:

MARCHENOIRE, THIS AUGUST 28,
IF YOU WANT TO LIVE, LEAVE MARCHENOIRE MANOR
IMMEDIATELY AND FOREVER. DO NOT PURCHASE THE
FORBIDDIN HOUSE

Perplexed, the grocer scratched his head.
He paced up and down the vast room, racking his brains.

The forbidden house....

What could it mean?

He recalled the old lawyer's curious reaction when Adhémar Dupont-Lesguyères had been the first to notice the strange missive on the mantelpiece.

'Don't touch it!' he had implored.

Nonetheless, Verdinage had opened the envelope. In his mind's eye, he could once again see Me. Laridoire shaking with fear, and the little clerk slumped against the wall, his legs weak, unable to utter a syllable.

He recalled also the uneasy attitude of the guard Bénard when the lawyer had introduced him as the future owner of Marchenoire.

The fat man aimed an irritated kick at a wastepaper basket whose contents were spread out on the ground.

'It's idiotic!' he exclaimed... 'We're not in the age of haunted castles and spectral ghosts any more!... It's just a joke in bad taste and nothing more... It had better stop right away, or the author will rue the day... I don't take kindly to being played for a fool.'

After a long, thoughtful silence, he murmured between clenched teeth:

'It's a joke... It's obviously a joke!'

After another silence, he sighed, unconvinced:

'But what if....?'

III

The next morning Verdinage woke up in a good mood.

It promised to be a beautiful day. The wind, which had blown gustily all night, had dropped completely. The sky, free of clouds, was radiantly blue.

'The good weather has returned,' said the fat man, and almost added: 'My servant the weather has cleansed my firmament and chased the rain far away from my property.'

But it was clear that was what he was thinking.

He rang for his valet to dress him in golfing clothes, the only attire—he believed—that an elegant country gentleman should sport.

He called for his secretary. Adhémar Dupont-Lesguyères came in, greeting him with a haughty correctness.

'Good morning, Marquis,' said the grocer. 'Is there anything of importance in this morning's mail?'

'Very little, monsieur. Two orders of pastry and an estimate from a supplier.'

'I'll look at it after I return. Before that, I'm going to take a walk in the village, which I haven't done yet.'

Adhémar bowed respectfully.

The owner put on a panama hat, which he wore comically perched on the back of his head, lit a cigar bearing an impressive gold band, and went out.

The village of Marchenoire had barely a hundred inhabitants, living in some forty small houses lining the road to Compiègne.

Several hundred metres from the village itself was a well-kept modern hostelry, looking like a cross between a thatched cottage and a plaster exhibition hall.

The Gothic sign proclaimed—with naïveté, irony, or cynicism— *l'Hostellerie du Coup de fusil, Anselme Chavignac, caterer.*

The prices posted were such as to discourage any local clientele; only passing motorists and the rich owners of the region bothered to cross the threshold of the *Coup de fusil.*

Verdinage consulted his gold chronometer. Noting that it was

21

already eleven o'clock, he sat down on the terrace and ordered an aperitif.

It seemed to him that the impeccable barman who came to take his order looked at him with an uneasy curiosity. After the man left, he could be seen whispering in the ear of the sommelier and nodding discreetly in the new owner's direction.

'What are they discussing?' thought Verdinage, who had noticed the conversation.

The words La Perrette had uttered to the housemaid- nanny came back to him—the same phrase which had been written on the typed letter and was now engraved in his memory.

Were they still talking about *the forbidden house?*

Irritated by the reminder, the fat man stood up, emptied his glass without pleasure, wiped his mouth with the back of his sleeve, and exited the *Coup de fusil,* leaving a big tip.

He strode purposefully towards the village.

His displeasure increased very soon, as it seemed to him—not without reason—that people whispered as he went past, and formed groups behind his back to talk in hushed tones. He had little doubt that he was their topic of conversation, which displeased him even more.

Nonetheless, overcoming his bad mood, he noticed an old man seated in full sunshine on a stone bench in front of his house door, smoking a pipe.

'Greetings, my good fellow,' said Verdinage amiably. 'Do you think we're in for a beautiful autumn?'

'It's possible,' replied the villager, expelling a stream of saliva.

And he added, after putting his pipe back in his mouth:

'Are you the new owner?'

'That's me!'

The old man shifted to the end of the bench and patted the space next to him.

'You can always sit down, you know.'

The grocer accepted the invitation.

Half an hour later, the two were the best of friends. The villager agreed, with undisguised pleasure, to sit with the new owner in the main room of the café *Ménard jeune.*

He told Verdinage that he was known as "le père Lafinette," that he was ninety years old, that he had been at the defeat of Tonkin, and was a retired customs officer.

Le père Lafinette, like many inhabitants of the region, was naturally taciturn, but became expansive after being plied with wine by his companion, and was soon chattering like a magpie.

Suddenly he frowned and stroked his moustache with a gnarled hand.

After coughing to hide his embarrassment, le père Lafinette became more solemn.

'You're a good fellow, and not proud, Monsieur Verdinage... But why the devil did you buy Marchenoire Manor? It's asking for trouble to live in the....'

He stopped as he saw the fat man's brow start to furrow, but the latter completed his thought:

'*The forbidden house*....That's what you were about to say, wasn't it, Père Lafinette? '

'Well... yes, Monsieur Verdinage. No offence... it's just the general opinion.'

'I'm well aware of that,' replied the grocer nervously. 'That's all I've heard since I bought the place. Let me assure you, it doesn't affect me one little bit.'

'Hell's Bells! A beautiful property like that. It would be a shame to leave it empty, wouldn't it?'

'You're right, Père Lafinette, and so I'm going to live there, despite the all the nonsense about a *forbidden house,* no matter how many jokers try to stop me.'

'Of course, Monsieur Verdinage, of course.'

'You at least, Père Lafinette, you don't believe that twaddle?'

'Ahum! Ahum!'

'Another white wine?'

'I don't mind if I do, Monsieur Verdinage. It's a nice drop.'

The old man gulped down the contents of his glass, clicked his tongue like a connoisseur, and tamped down his pipe as he muttered:

'It's a beautiful property, to be sure, only....'

'Only....' repeated Verdinage.

Le père Lafinette seemed embarrassed. If he hadn't lost his self-control as a result of the multiple tipples, he might not have continued his ramblings.

After a short hesitation, he continued in a thick voice:

'It's not enough to have bought Marchenoire Manor, Monsieur Verdinage... *You have to be able to stay in it.*'

'But, Père Lafinette, I have every intention to do so, because I've installed myself and all my servants, and I defy anyone to make me leave until I decide to do so.'

'Who knows, Monsieur Verdinage? Who knows?'

'I defy—.'

'Don't defy anyone.'

'And why not?'

'*Because you'll be just like the others.*'

'Which others?'

'The other owners of the manor. They left... *you'll leave, just like them.*'

The fat man sneered:

'Ah, yes! Because of the letter... the famous threatening letter.'

'That's right,' murmured the villager, lowering his voice.

Verdinage looked at the other in astonishment.

'You know that I've received a letter?'

Le père Lafinette tapped the bowl of his pipe on the sole of his shoe and declared:

'I know it... I also know that you found it on the mantelpiece of the stone fireplace in the library.'

The grocer stammered:

'But who told you?'

'Nobody, I tell you. Nobody! I know *because it always happens in the same way.*'

'Wait a moment! Wait a moment,' choked the owner, now becoming truly concerned. 'And if I ignore the instruction in the letter, and stay anyway, what will happen to me?'

'Then... Dammit!'

Le père Lafinette stopped talking. He made a gesture to indicate he didn't want to continue.

Verdinage insisted, breathing heavily.

'Then what? What?'

The old man spoke clearly and slowly:

'*Then something bad will happen to you.*'

The fat man rubbed his eyes as if trying to forget a horrible

24

nightmare.

He started to reflect, and the more he thought about it, the more he was forced to admit that a mystery surrounded Marchenoire Manor, a mystery the whole village knew about, and a mystery Me. Laridoire had concealed from him.

When he, Verdinage, after visiting the manor, had expressed his intention to sign the purchase contract in the library, the old lawyer had looked startled.

He'd looked startled because he knew that the grocer would find the letter there.

He'd been afraid that the threat in the letter would influence his client and prevent the completion of a difficult sale.

Marchenoire Manor was a vast property, comfortable and admirably situated.

Yet, despite its extremely low price, it had remained practically abandoned for several months without attracting a single buyer.

There had to be a reason for such a lack of interest.

No one wanted to buy Marchenoire Manor, despite its charm and low price, *because it was forbidden*, because no owner could *keep the forbidden house.*

IV

Having replenished the drinks, Verdinage didn't have to wait long for le père Lafinette to continue his confidences.

The old man, whose eyes watered easily under the influence of alcohol, sat straight up in his chair, tried to look important, and continued:

'I know the story of the manor from the very beginning. I saw it being built, just over five years ago, for the famous banker Abraham Goldenberg.'

'Goldenberg?' repeated the grocer in astonishment. 'The Goldenberg of *Crédit Continental*?'

'The same. A friendly, chatty man, despite his millions... A bit like you, Monsieur Verdinage.'

'Thank you,' replied Verdinage tersely, not finding the comparison to his taste.

The founder of the *Société du Crédit Continental*, which had distributed large dividends from its beginning, boasted the support of numerous financial institutions, whose assets it insured.

One day they were all dumbfounded to learn that the banker had disappeared, leaving debts of twenty-five million francs.

The swindle affected not only the magnates of finance, but also a multitude of small investors, many of whom were ruined and committed suicide in despair.

Abraham Goldenberg was arrested just as he was about to embark on a voyage to South America.

His trial was long and eventful. The magistrates were unsuccessful in getting him to confess how he had spent the missing millions. He spoke of unfortunate speculations, but never provided proof.

Sentenced to seven years' hard labour, he accepted the sentence with disdain, in the mistaken belief that the influence of certain politicians would allow him to escape punishment.

He died two months after starting his sentence.

His wife, who had stood by him during the trial, poisoned herself upon learning of his death.

It was understandable that Verdinage did not feel flattered by le père Lafinette's comparison.

'I'm sorry,' stuttered the old man. 'I know, for the love of God, that the banker came to a sticky end... but he seemed like such a decent gentleman that nobody would have suspected that of him.

'Getting back to Marchenoire Manor, it was put up for sale after the death of Goldenberg and his wife, but the price was a pittance compared to the millions stolen by the banker.

'It was purchased by a certain M. Desrousseaux and it was *from that moment on that the "things" started happening.'*

The old peasant paused. The grocer took the opportunity to pour another copious glassful of white wine and encourage him to continue his account:

'So, as you were saying, Père Lafinette, this M. Desrousseaux bought Marchenoire Manor...'

'It was just the same!... He hadn't lived there a week before the first letter arrived. He found it in on the mantelpiece of the stone fireplace in the library.'

'Just like me, but mine was delivered before I'd even signed the purchase contract,' observed Verdinage.

'One month after receiving the first letter, M. Desrousseaux received another one, and, after another month, he received a third. He took no notice, thinking it was a joke. One day they found him lying in the park, near the fountain, dead from a rifle shot.'

'But surely they tried to find the author of the threatening letters, and looked into the private life of the victim?' asked the new owner anxiously.

'They did all that and more, Monsieur Verdinage, and they found nothing. M. Desrousseaux was a gentle man who didn't appear to have any enemies. And yet he was murdered. It happened at nightfall: M. Desrousseaux had gone out for a walk before dinner. His family and the servants, who had remained in the house, heard the shot clearly. They assumed that the poor man, who was a passionate hunter, had shot a pheasant in the forest of l'Aigle. Everyone was interrogated: Bénard, the guard—who, having been in the service of the Goldenbergs, had been inherited by M. Desrousseaux—was unable to provide any useful information to help the police in their enquiries. Eventually, the examining magistrate closed the case.'

'It's inconceivable!' retorted Verdinage. 'If M. Desrousseaux hadn't any enemies, it must mean that his death profited someone. Did they look into that?'

'I repeat, they looked into everything. Everything! M. Desrousseaux was a widower. His heirs were his children, two little boys and a little girl he adored.

'Besides, the threatening letters addressed to him only demanded one thing, and always the same: *that he leave.*'

'It's extraordinary,' gasped the grocer, now as white as a sheet. Drops of sweat rolled down his chubby face. He was impatient to learn more, *to know everything.* He asked fearfully:

'After. What happened after the murder?'

'Afterwards the guardian put the château up for sale, because of the minors. They found a buyer and the business of the threatening letters began all over again.'

'The business of the letters began again?'

'Exactly. The new lord of the manor had hardly moved in before finding the first letter on the library mantelpiece, and then another one thirty days later informing him that he would be killed, just like his predecessor, if he persisted in occupying... *the forbidden house.*

'He understood that M. Desrousseaux had died because he had continued to live in the manor *despite the order to leave.* He understood that the other man's murder was for no other reason than his obstinacy, because he, the new owner, had been threatened *in exactly the same language.*'

'And what happened to that gentleman?'

'Nothing!... Nothing, because he was wise enough to pack his bags and leave before the third letter arrived, so Me. Laridoire put *the forbidden house* up for sale yet again.'

'And was a buyer found straight away?'

'Not straight away, because news of the letters had started to spread and was the subject of much gossip. Nevertheless, an industrialist from Senlis did buy it, but he became frightened when he received the first letter and left immediately.

'Since then, there have been two others, both gentlemen from Paris whose names we never knew because they, too, preferred to leave after the first letter, to avoid the fate of poor M. Desrousseaux.'

Verdinage was thinking.

The history of Marchenoire Manor wasn't as tragic as le père Lafinette had made it out to be. Goldenberg, the first owner, who died in prison, got his just deserts. Only Desrousseaux had been murdered. All the others had left, frightened by the anonymous letters, but there was nothing to prove that the threats would have been carried out by the writer. There was nothing to prove that it was he who had killed Desrousseaux, for that matter. Maybe the latter's tragic death after the first letters was nothing but a simple coincidence, exploited by a demented letter-writer to terrorise successive owners.

Hadn't there been many examples already of maniacs deriving unhealthy pleasure from creating panic in their village by sending anonymous, abusive or threatening letters to prominent fellow-citizens?

In such cases, uncovering the culprit was a long and delicate process. An appearance of honesty and respectability deflected suspicion, until they were actually caught in the act, threatening or sending.

Verdinage, deciding he had had quite enough of le père Lafinette, settled the bill and left.

He made his way back to the manor, stopping occasionally to raise his panama hat and wipe the sweat from his flushed forehead.

As he passed a group of women, he heard one of them say to the others:

'There goes the new lord of the manor. He's so obstinate! He doesn't want to leave... But he'll go anyway... in a hearse!'

Several of her companions crossed themselves.

Verdinage crossed the park, ignoring Clodoche's greeting, went quickly into the manor, and burst into the library.

Adhémar was sitting in front of a typewriter, working on the grocer's correspondence.

The elegant secretary got up and asked his boss if he had had an enjoyable walk.

Verdinage uttered a coarse grunt and slumped down in an armchair.

Adhémar was surprised by such an attitude. He'd become accustomed to see Verdinage smiling and cordial.

'If the *nouveau-riche* becomes disagreeable,' grumbled the Adonis to himself, 'the place will become unbearable.'

'Here's the correspondence, signed,' offered the fat man tersely, so pre-occupied that he forgot to address the other by his title.

Just at that moment, someone tapped timidly at the door.

'Come in,' said Verdinage in a disdainful tone.

Gustave Colinet appeared.

'What do you want?' asked the lord of the manor.

'M. Bénard would like to speak to you privately,' replied the valet solemnly.

'What does he want?'

'I didn't permit myself to ask.'

'Very well. Send him in.'

Gustave waved the guard in and left. Bénard advanced awkwardly, cap in hand.

'Monsieur,' he began, 'I'm sorry to bother you, but I felt it was important... because I mustn't wait to tell you... what I have to say.'

He stopped and cast an eye at the secretary, who was listening.

Verdinage turned to Adhémar Dupont-Lesguyères and told him:

'Marquis, I invite you to go into the hall for a smoke, to take your mind off things.'

Annoyed to have been ordered out, the other placed the cover on the typewriter and left in a dignified manner.

The grocer lit a cigar.

'Speak up, Bénard. I'm listening.'

'Here's the thing, monsieur... I haven't any advice to give you, of course... You're free to do as you wish... And I'm very pleased to be in your service because we seem to get on very well... at least, I think so... but... but....'

'But you want to leave?' cut in Verdinage, expelling a cloud of smoke.

'No, monsieur... not me!'

'You want me to fire someone?... Clodoche?'

'Oh no, monsieur.'

'You surely don't think that, just to be agreeable to my guard, I'm going to fire one of my servants?... I've known them all for years and I'm happy with their service... It's not you, Bénard, who has only recently been engaged, that's going to—.'

'That's not what I'm trying to say, monsieur.'

'Then explain yourself, for heaven's sake! Who do you want to leave?'

'You, monsieur!'

Stupefied, Verdinage almost swallowed his cigar. He erupted:

'You're mad, Bénard. Stark raving mad!'

'No, monsieur! But....'

'You're not making any sense.'

'Monsieur, *you have to leave!*'

'Not on your life... You're all a bunch of idiots with your stories about letters and *the forbidden house*... "I'm here and I'm staying," as someone I can't remember said.'

'You're wrong, monsieur!... You have to leave... *you have to leave before something bad happens.*'

V

Three weeks went by. It was the end of September. Rust-coloured leaves covered the paths of the park.

Verdinage had restored the kennels next door to the guardhouse. Twelve superb Great Danes had been housed there. The magnificent muzzled creatures filled the air with their loud barking.

They frightened Clodoche at first, but, little by little, the cripple became emboldened. Soon, he seemed to take pleasure in looking after them and would allow no one else to take them their food twice a day.

Bénard made no attempt to challenge him and Verdinage deduced from that detail—and many others—that the guard was extremely lazy, working very little and forcing the unfortunate cripple to perform all the menial tasks.

It became clear that, in recruiting Clodoche, Bénard's intention had been to use him as a beast of burden, which cast a dubious light on his seeming act of charity.

Too stupid to protest, the cripple struggled without complaining, ate little and drank even less, just happy, after a day's hard labour, to collapse onto the hard, flat, straw mattress the guard had left for him in the far corner of the guardhouse.

Clodoche was less well fed and nourished than the dogs he looked after.

Verdinage, who felt sorry for him, sought him out often for a chat. The conversation consisted mainly of Clodoche nodding his head and grunting, whilst the grocer did almost all of the talking. In fact, he preferred talking alone, or almost, to conversing with his secretary, who was only too ready to point out any incorrect use of language.

After his last discussion with the guard, the lord of the manor had only addressed him in order to convey instructions. He was coming to dislike Bénard more and more.

He remembered their last conversation in the library, where the guard assured him several times that he was only acting in his master's interests. Verdinage was astonished by the obstinacy with which Bénard had repeated:

'You must leave!... You must leave!'

That insolent insistence displeased Verdinage. Far from persuading him to go, it had reinforced his decision to stay. It was a question of self-respect.

He even thought about sacking this guard who guarded nothing and whose only skill lay in exploiting the misery and ignorance of the unfortunate Clodoche. To that end, he was waiting for his indolent servant to commit a flagrant misstep.

But Bénard, whose principal occupation seemed to consist of walking in the park or the surrounding area, was careful not to commit any error of the sort.

In any case, a distressing incident diverted the owner's attention.

Since his arrival at Marchenoire, the butler, Charles Chapon, had devoted an excessive amount of his time to his favourite vice.

He only performed his duties grudgingly, serving clumsily at table, neglecting to serve his master bread, and failing to burnish the cutlery—previously sparkling and now dull and dirty.

The cellar, on the other hand, gained the full attention of the husband of "housemaid-nanny," who had discovered in the dusty space a considerable stock of vintage Pommard, left behind by the banker Goldenberg.

Verdinage loved his old butler, in whom he had absolute confidence. But, on several occasions, Charles showed signs of intoxication too obvious for the lord of the manor not to notice.

He lectured Charles affectionately until the latter broke down in tears and confessed his frequent visits to the cellar and repeated indulgence in libations.

When the butler, carrying a dish on which sat a turkey artistically prepared by Jeanne, tripped on the carpet and sprawled full length on the dining room floor, the grocer could no longer contain himself and exploded.

All the servants heard the diatribe that Verdinage unleashed upon the drunk.

The fat man's voice resonated up to the rafters, whilst the pitiful culprit sobbed and sniffed in turns.

'I've had enough!... Enough!' shouted Verdinage, pounding the table so hard that the crockery and cutlery shook. 'Do you understand me, animal? ... I know very well that you're constantly drinking my wines and liqueurs!... I'm rich enough that these petty thefts don't affect me... But what I cannot tolerate is to see you in your present state!... I can't accept that... I've shut my eyes up until now, not so much for you as for your poor wife... You're lucky that Thérèse raised me. But for that, I would have kicked you out a long time ago!'

There was a silence, during which Charles's sobs doubled in intensity.

The lord of the manor began again in a calmer voice:

'I'm warning you that the first time you get drunk, the first time, do you hear, I will throw you out without hesitation!... Do you realise what you'll lose if it ever comes to that?... You know I'm a bachelor and my only relatives are distant cousins, whom I care as little about as they care for me, which is saying a lot!'

Verdinage spoke slowly, emphasizing each word:

'You and your wife are my principal heirs. The fortune of old Verdinage is quite something, isn't it? Well, as my name is Napoléon and yours is Charles, if I throw you out, I will disinherit both of you at the same time. All I have to do is drop my solicitor a line for my will to be annulled... Do you understand? Annulled. You won't get a sou and you'll die in hospital... Too bad, it will be your own doing... Take a nap and sleep on it... Tomorrow morning, you'll come and tell me you've decided to conduct yourself properly from now on, or else ... Now go and sleep!'

The grocer grabbed the butler by the shoulders and pushed him out of the dining room. Charles staggered to the office and collapsed. His wife was waiting for him and gave him a tongue-lashing, beside which Verdinage's own was a mere joke.

Thérèse swore in a low voice so that her tirade did not reach the lord of the manor's ears.

In vain did Edmond and Jeanne Tasseau—the chauffeur and the cook—try to calm the unhinged housemaid-nanny. They only succeeded in getting a fresh torrent of abuse heaped on Charles.

Verdinage, having lost his appetite because of the violent scene, frowned as he sat gloomily opposite Adhémar Dupont-Lesguyères, who dared not break the silence.

Meanwhile, the valet Gustave Colinet quietly took over the butler's duties whilst the latter suffered his interminable humiliation.

The following morning, Charles sheepishly appeared before the lord of the manor, his head hung low.

Verdinage, who had got a good night's sleep, placed a large hand paternally on the butler's shoulder.

'So, do you swear?' he asked. 'Do I have your word? Excellent!'

'Monsieur is too kind to me,' murmured the drunkard, staring at the floor.

Jocularly, the grocer added:

'Go back to work, you scoundrel, and make sure you leave me a few bottles of that vintage Pommard the late Goldenberg so fortuitously left behind.'

Charles, repentant and with a voice choked with emotion, replied:

'I promise Monsieur that I will not set foot in the cellar except in Monsieur's service.'

'Well then,' concluded his master with a laugh, 'you'd better go there now, because lunch is almost ready.'

The butler bowed, mumbled some vague thanks, and left.

A few minutes later, just as Verdinage was about to partake of a bowl of rich chocolate, Charles reappeared, wild-eyed. He was as white as a sheet, and in his hand he clutched an envelope.

'Who gave you that?' asked the grocer, as he snatched the missive out of his hands.

'Nobody, Monsieur, nobody.'

'Have you been drinking again, by any chance?'

'Oh no, Monsieur!... Monsieur can't possibly think that... As I said, nobody gave me that envelope... I found it.'

'Where did you find it?'

'On the first step leading down to the cellar.'

'But no one but you has the key to the cellar!'

'*That's why I'm frightened*, Monsieur... That letter wasn't there yesterday evening... I would have noticed it.'

'You were too drunk for that!'

'Exactly, Monsieur.'

'What do you mean?'

'When I'm... what Monsieur says... I look where I put my feet, for fear of falling... and so I would have seen the letter on the step... I

36

couldn't have missed it! And, this morning, it was the first thing I saw.'

'Someone probably slipped it under the door.'

'Impossible, Monsieur. The door is a very tight fit at the bottom. It's actually quite hard to open. You couldn't thread a hair under it.'

'Are you sure you locked the door last night?'

'I couldn't be more sure, Monsieur. Not only did I shoot the bolt, I turned the key twice in the lock.'

'And this morning, the door was just as you left it?'

'Yes, Monsieur.'

Verdinage turned the mysterious missive over and over in his fingers.

An address had been typed on the envelope.

Monsieur Napoléon VERDINAGE
Marchenoire Manor,
near Compiègne   (Oise)

The grocer fell silent for a moment.

He dismissed the butler with a sign, whereupon the latter announced to the world that he had picked up a letter from an unknown person from the first step of the cellar, despite a locked and bolted door and wire mesh on the windows!

Verdinage looked at a calendar on the wall.

"Today is the 28th of September . It's exactly one month since... *He's accurate!"* he said to himself.

He tore open the envelope.

It was indeed the threat he had expected.

He read:

MARCHENOIRE, THIS SEPTEMBER 28,
THIS IS THE SECOND AND LAST WARNING. THERE IS
STILL TIME TO OBEY ME AND LEAVE THE FORBIDDIN
HOUSE.
IF, IN ONE MONTH, OCTOBER 28, YOU ARE STILL HERE,
YOU WILL RECEIVE A THIRD LETTER, BUT IT WILL
CONTAIN THE ANNOUNCEMENT OF YOUR DEATH. YOU

HAVE THIRTY DAYS TO REFLECT. ONCE THAT DELAY IS PAST, IT WILL BE TOO LATE.

YOUR BEHAVIOUR WILL DECIDE YOUR FATE. YOU WILL LEAVE THE MANOR DEAD OR ALIVE.

VI

Upon the receipt of the second anonymous letter, Verdinage had felt a shiver of fear run up his spine. He had considered at length whether it would indeed be wiser to leave the premises, rather than risk death by staying.

Then he laughed at his fears, chastised himself for thinking like a coward, and decided to stay in the manor, come what may.

He was strolling thoughtfully along one of the paths in the park when he chanced to see Bénard.

The guard ran towards his master as soon as he noticed him.

'Monsieur, I just heard the news.'

'What news?' asked the grocer gruffly.

'I know you've received the second letter.'

'You're well informed.'

'I'm sorry. That's the talk of the village everywhere. I just came from the cafe *Ménard jeune*, where the news is being widely discussed.'

'Charles has been very discrete,' said Verdinage sarcastically, furious to have provoked such an emotion.

'What do you plan to do, monsieur?'

'That's none of your business!'

'Of course, monsieur... But, just think, if you're still here in Marchenoire one month from now, you will receive a third letter... and the end will be near.'

The owner stared hard at the guard's face.

'Ah, monsieur,' the man repeated, 'how I wish it were not so. I can see what will happen because I remember what occurred at the time of poor Monsieur Desrousseaux, the first owner of the manor after the death of M. and Mme. Goldenberg... I was here, monsieur!'

'You were here...,' repeated Verdinage.

'I shall never forget that horrible tragedy... M. Desrousseaux showed me the two letters which had arrived a month apart, and we had a good laugh. At the time, I didn't realise it was serious. Another month passed... the third letter arrived, and....'

'I know! I know!' The grocer cut him off impatiently.

He asked the guard point blank:

'And was it a rifle shot that killed Desrousseaux?'

'Yes, monsieur.'

'And were you with your master when the *accident* happened?'

He had intentionally stressed the word "accident," which seemed to disconcert Bénard. The guard replied in a hoarse, unsteady voice:

'No, monsieur... No... I....'

Verdinage questioned him brutally:

'What were you doing?... Eh?... Answer me!'

'I was... I was out walking in the Aigle forest... Quite a long way from here.'

'And did you warn the subsequent buyers of the danger—or supposed danger—that they would be running?'

'Me. Laridoire didn't do it, so it wasn't up to me to be more forthcoming... Nevertheless, when the first letter arrived, I acted according to my conscience... Just as I did with the other owners.'

'I wonder how many of them were weak enough to listen to you.'

'I'm glad I did it, monsieur. Thanks to me there have been no deadly incidents since the murder of M. Desrousseaux. Each time I've seen one of my masters follow my advice and leave here, it's relieved a burden I have here, in my heart.'

'You're such a good fellow,' sneered the lord of the manor. 'As far as I'm concerned, I order you to leave me alone, otherwise one of us will shortly be leaving Marchenoire, and it won't be me!'

'Yes, monsieur... But permit me once more—.'

'I don't permit anything! I'll do what I feel like! *And I'll have you know that I find your desire to make me leave my own property very suspicious.*'

Bénard went pale. Verdinage angrily turned his back.

The guard continued in a low voice:

'I did what I could. I hope that a month from now you will have thought about it.'

Losing all patience, the grocer turned around and shouted:

'You're a nuisance, do you understand! I'm sick and tired of your stories. Someone wants to frighten me, Napoléon Verdinage, executive director of the grocers' association of Montrouge! You and your kind need to learn that I'm not afraid of anyone, and threats of this nature won't affect a man of my mettle!... My anonymous correspondent has been kind enough to give me one month to think about it... One month!... I've never needed a month to make a decision!... I'm not leaving, and I won't have changed my mind come next October 28th. That's it. I have spoken!'

Bénard, stunned by the sudden explosion of wrath, watched the lord of the manor walk away at a rapid pace.

....

If fear is infectious, then so are assurance and self-confidence . Gradually, calm returned to Marchenoire Manor.

Favourably impressed by the attitude of their master, the servants no longer showed the fear which had gripped them the month before.

They did speak amongst themselves, of course, about the famous letter that Charles had found, but it was only to ask themselves out of curiosity how it had appeared there, on the top step of the cellar stairs.

They also knew, from experience, that any allusion to the mysterious letters resulted in Verdinage becoming very exasperated, which caused all those around him to suffer.

So they waited until their master was away before discussing it quietly amongst themselves.

It had drizzled incessantly for about a week.

Confined to the manor, Verdinage looked out through the high windows of the library at the vast park covered in mist.

'Bloody weather,' he grumbled. 'I can't even go out for my daily walk.'

He rang for his chauffeur and ordered him to get his limousine ready. Soon he heard the motor of the powerful vehicle throbbing outside the front entrance.

Just as the owner was about to climb into the car, the postman, dripping wet, brought him a pile of letters.

'Take them,' said Verdinage to Dupont-Lesguyères, who was behind him. 'We can open them in the car. That will give us something to do... Postman, go into the kitchen and drink a glass of mulled wine to my health.'

41

'With pleasure, M'sieur Verdinage,' replied the good fellow, tipping his kepi. 'This cursed rain makes you cold inside!'

So saying, he watched the shining limousine with a mixture of admiration and envy, as it pulled smoothly away in the capable hands of Edmond Tasseau.

....

The postman, comfortably installed in the kitchen, seemed in no hurry to confront the elements again. He drank his mulled wine in small sips, accompanying each with a satisfied chuckle.

He sighed as he watched the glass panes washed by the rain and chatted with Jeanne the cook, whom Gustave, the valet, was helping to peel the broad beans for lunch.

Soon Charles and Thérèse joined them and the tongues started wagging.

And what else could they talk about but the story which, for two months, had been the talk of the village: the threatening letters received by their master?

'It's all very strange,' observed the postman, shaking his head.

'Speaking personally,' intervened the butler, 'I'm still trying to work out how anyone could have put the second letter on the top step of the cellar stairs, when the door was well and truly locked.'

'Shut up, you old drunk!' snorted Thérèse, giving him a sharp jab in the ribs. 'You were as pissed as a newt the night before and you simply forgot that you never locked the cellar door.'

'That's not true, Madame Thérèse,' said Jeanne. 'Because the next day M. Charles had to draw the bolt and turn the key twice, which means the cellar door was locked.'

'Jeanne is right!' agreed Charles self-righteously. 'It's a complete mystery, as they say in detective novels.'

'And you? What do you think?' the postman asked the valet, who was listening to the others, but had not yet joined in the conversation.

'Me?' replied Gustave Colinet, who had not lost his habitual calm. 'I haven't got an opinion.'

The rain stopped for a moment. The postman emptied his glass in one gulp and took his leave regretfully, saying goodbye to each of "messieurs-dames" in turn.

He put on his cape, made heavier by the rain, as he told himself that the servants of M. Verdinage really had a soft life.

....

The grocer's car, as shiny as a waxed floor, proceeded at a modest speed towards Compiègne.

Seated comfortably in the wide rear seat, Verdinage had placed his feet on the foldaway seat opposite.

Adhémar Dupont-Lesguyères was opening the envelopes with the aid of a small penknife bearing the family coat of arms, reading the contents quickly and summarising them for his master.

The latter dictated the gist of his reply immediately, which the young secretary took down in shorthand on the notepad that never left his side.

The lord of the manor had lit a cigar and was blowing clouds of smoke in the face of the Adonis, who coughed and sneezed until his eyes watered, but did not dare complain.

'An order from Pressoir Entreprises,' mumbled Adhémar.

'How much?'

'Six thousand tins of Pâtes Verdinages.'

'Approved! Send the order to the factory. Next?'

'An offer from the firm of Kirweis and Schwartz, of Hamburg,'

'Worthwhile?'

'Kirweis and Schwartz are fine with the quality. The price remains to be seen.'

'Refer to Technical Services with instructions to get references. Next?'

Not receiving a response, Verdinage turned to look at his secretary.

Adhémar's normally pale face had turned a shade of green. Unable to utter a word, the young man handed his master a typed letter.

Verdinage seized it and read the lines which seemed to dance on the onion paper:

MARCHENOIRE, THIS OCTOBER 28.

THE MONTH HAS PASSED.
YOU HAVE NOT WANTED TO LEAVE THE FORBIDDIN

HOUSE.
IT IS NOW TOO LATE TO CHANGE YOUR MIND.
TONIGHT, AT AROUND MIDNIGHT, I WILL COME TO
MARCHENOIRE MANOR AND I WILL KILL YOU.

The grocer went green in turn.

And so. the author of the two previous letters was speaking. He was sending, on the appointed date, the last missive containing the death warrant.

'Back to the manor!' shouted Verdinage to the driver.

The car slowed, turned, and shot off at high speed in the direction of Marchenoire.

His head between his hands, the lord of the manor was thinking frantically.

Should he run away?

Should he yield to the threat and play the game of this stranger who presumed to give him orders?

The idea appalled him.

What the Hell? You didn't go around murdering people who couldn't defend themselves.

Verdinage thought about filing a complaint in Compiègne and having the police guard his property. He told himself, with reason, that his adversary would have thought of that and would be sure not to make an appearance if he saw unusual activity around the manor.

The would-be assassin would simply postpone his project to a more favourable moment, and the peril would merely be delayed.

Because the unknown assailant had been impudent enough to specify the precise hour of the attack, it would be better to stand firm and try to find an explanation as to why this audacious criminal wanted Marchenoire Manor *to remain unoccupied*.

For the same reason, Verdinage wanted to make sure that the servants remained unaware of the third letter.

If the staff were alerted—and the visitor would have thought of that as well—the nocturnal meeting would not take place: not wishing to stick his head in the lion's mouth, the author of the anonymous letters would remain hidden, content to kill the lord of the manor from a distance, with a rifle shot for example, as he had done for Desrousseaux.

44

It would be better to arrange a tête-à-tête and confront him bravely in secret, man to man, in order to rid him of his tyrannical obsession.

Verdinage was strong and determined. He feared no one. Just to be safe, he would have a loaded revolver within easy reach.

In addition, the five people living in the manor would be on their feet at the first call; Bénard and Clodoche, who inhabited the guardhouse, would rush to the aid of their master and bar the retreat of the fugitive.

Besides, the whole business might just be a bad joke.

By the time the limousine reached the front gate of the park, the grocer had formulated his plan.

He asked his secretary, who was still shaking, to follow him into the library, where he carefully closed the door.

'Marquis,' he said calmly, 'you are not to tell anyone that I received a new threatening letter this morning. I don't want the manor to be overcome by fear again. That would guarantee that I wouldn't be able to count on any of the servants... Get a hold of yourself! Act in such a way that no one suspects anything. You asked me this morning for permission to go to the county ball, and I approved. So you won't be here tonight and you have nothing to fear personally.'

Adhémar Dupont-Lesguyères promised to do what his master had asked and took refuge in his room, so as not to let the servants get a glimpse of his ashen countenance.

Now alone, Verdinage leant against the stone mantelpiece and, as he always did when he was upset, talked to himself:

"It's decided, then!... You will stay and await the arrival of your adversary around midnight... All the same, it would be foolhardy to expose yourself to shots in the night by walking around in the park... Better to send someone to bring your enemy here... You will open the door yourself noiselessly, so as not to awaken the flunkeys sleeping upstairs... Very well, then, whom to send to the park gate? Adhémar will be away... If you designate Edmond, he will talk to Jeanne and then the whole countryside will know... Eliminate Charles for the same reason... That leaves Gustave, who's too insignificant to carry out such an important task... So then... Bénard?

"Ah, no! Not him!... In that case, Clodoche? Not him either, he's an idiot and a cripple... What irony! Napoléon, old boy, you're surrounded by numerous well-trained staff, but in reality, you're

45

isolated in your own manor, because you can't count on any of them! Nevertheless, tonight, you will have to meet the one who has ordered you to leave *the forbidden house.*

"Adhémar Dupont-Lesguyères, Edmond Tasseau, Charles Chapon, Gustave Colinet, Bénard, Clodoche... All imbeciles!... All useless!... All cowards! ... You're badly served, my poor Napoléon... What's the point of being rich? Everything is just vanity, as the marquis, your secretary, claims."

For a long time, the *nouveau-riche* continued his monologue, pitying his misfortune:

"Make a decision, my poor Napoléon. First of all, if you don't want to be shot like a rabbit at the gate of your own manor, you will receive the one who is threatening you in the library... You have a Browning, the latest model, and you can fire at the first suspicious gesture... Of course. Of course. But for that to happen, someone has to meet the visitor at the gate, because you've decided not to go yourself. The criminal will only come if he's accompanied and assured of your peaceful intentions... So one of your servants must wait for him at the park gate... but which one? Bah! Just as the marquis said: it's the least of all the evils."

Frowning from the effort, Verdinage once again went through the list of servants in his head. He mulled over two of the names: Charles Chapon and Edmond Tasseau.

"Those two," he said to himself, "are the only ones who could accomplish such a delicate mission. Let me see: Charles Chapon or Edmond Tasseau? My butler or my chauffeur?"

He made a gesture of annoyance and continued with his soliloquy:

"To send either of those imbeciles would be a mistake. Yes, Napoléon, old boy, a mistake. The wives of those two idiots lead them around by the nose! ... At midnight, instead of being asleep, all the servants would be awake, alerted by the indiscretions of those two gossips. My anticipated visitor would have quickly realised what was going on—he knows everything, sees everything, and hears everything—and he would simply not turn up. And then, Napoléon, old boy, you would never solve the mystery of *the forbidden house.* So, neither Chapon nor Tasseau!"

Working his way through the list of servants, Napoléon Verdinage continued:

"... nor Clodoche, nor Bénard... That leaves Gustave Colinet, your valet."

The *nouveau-riche* laughed out loud thinking about the insignificant figure of Gustave Colinet:

"He would be the absolute last choice. He's afraid of his own shadow, and the slightest rustling of the leaves in the park would cause him to faint from terror!"

He stopped laughing abruptly as he thought about his guard again.

"Jacques Bénard," he murmured to himself. "Obviously someone like that is used to roaming around at night, and a poacher—or worse!—wouldn't cause him to back off, but his terror of the mysterious letter writer seems to affect him too much."

Verdinage hesitated for a moment, and then concluded:

"There's another reason not to give him an important mission: he's a shady character and I don't trust him one bit. Not an inch!"

The fat man shook his head in disillusionment. He was pouting like a spoilt baby, just about to cry.

An idea which had been lurking in the back of his mind came to the surface and he murmured:

"After all, why not?... Why not Clodoche? He's stupider than all the rest put together, but isn't that precisely what makes him perfect for the job?... The idiot wouldn't understand anything or ask for any explanations. He would simply obey, like the oaf he is! Despite his gammy leg, he's strong enough to come to your aid if necessary. All you have to do is teach him word by word what you need him to say to whomever turns up at the gate. He doesn't need to understand it. All he has to do is bring him to me and I'll do the rest... I'll tell him to stay on the front steps, like a good guard dog, and whack anyone with his crutch who leaves without my consent. Napoléon, old boy, I think you've finally found the ideal solution!"

....

The grocer ate a hearty breakfast, smoked a Havana cigar, and took advantage of a sunny spell to walk down to the fountain.

Clodoche was there, raking out the bottom of the basin, and emptying stagnant water out with a pail.

Verdinage touched the cripple lightly on the shoulder. The latter gave a slight start, then smiled as he recognised his master.

'My dear old Clodoche,' said the lord of the manor. 'We need to have a serious talk. Stop what you're doing, particularly since it's about to rain and you'll have to start all over again tomorrow.'

Walking slowly so that the other could follow, Verdinage led Clodoche to an out of the way spot and told him what he wanted him to do.

The idiot opened his eyes wide, frowned, and eventually nodded his head solemnly.

The grocer repeated his instructions several times and ordered his servant to repeat them.

In a hoarse voice, Clodoche articulated slowly:

'Tonight... midnight... Clodoche hides near gate... Someone comes... Clodoche leads "the someone" with his lantern up to the manor. Monsieur opens the door and Clodoche waits on the steps... If Clodoche hears a noise inside, he calls for help... If Clodoche hears nothing, he stays where he is... When "the someone" leaves, Clodoche takes him back to the gate... But Clodoche doesn't let "the someone" leave if Clodoche has heard a noise, or if Monsieur says, "Stop him!"'

....

Verdinage went back to the manor.

He read several newspapers whilst waiting for dinner, then ate quickly, to the despair of Jeanne, who had taken particular care to prepare a sumptuous meal.

At ten o'clock, he went ostentatiously upstairs to sleep.

Just before midnight, he got up surreptitiously and dressed.

Everyone was asleep in the silent manor.

Outside, the wind was blowing hard, bringing gusts of rain.

The grocer took a Browning from the bedside table and verified that it was loaded.

He went down the stairs cautiously, grateful that the thick carpet muffled his steps completely.

He tiptoed through the entrance hall and entered the library.

After drawing the curtains noiselessly, so that no light would escape, even from the edges, he turned on the lights to illuminate the vast room.

His watch showed ten minutes to midnight.

He waited.

Verdinage opened a drawer and retrieved the letter he had received that very morning, and slowly re-read the text:

MARCHENOIRE, THIS OCTOBER 28.

THE MONTH HAS PASSED.

YOU HAVE NOT WANTED TO LEAVE THE FORBIDDIN HOUSE.

IT IS NOW TOO LATE TO CHANGE YOUR MIND.

TONIGHT, AT AROUND MIDNIGHT, I WILL COME TO MARCHENOIRE MANOR AND I WILL KILL YOU.

The grocer looked at his watch again.

A quarter past twelve....

He picked up a pencil and scrawled offhandedly across the foot of the threatening letter:

"A quarter past twelve... Nothing."

Adhémar Dupont-Lesguyères kept his word and did not reveal the secret with which he had been entrusted.

Feigning migraine, he had been served a light dinner in his room and then, at around half past nine, had slipped quietly out of Marchenoire Manor, without anyone seeing him leave.

He passed through the gate with a sense of relief and walked rapidly towards the village, casting a furtive look back from time to time.

To a passing stranger, he would have given the impression of a fugitive on the run, rather than an inoffensive adolescent attending a ball.

To tell the truth, he hurried, not so much as to arrive quickly at his destination, but more to distance himself as quickly as possible from the manor, over which hung a frightening mystery.

....

When Verdinage, after going up to his bedroom, had descended stealthily into the library to wait for the anonymous letter writer, he had believed that everyone else in the manor was asleep.

The lord of the manor was wrong.

Two people were keeping watch: Thérèse Chapon on the ground floor, and Gustave Colinet in the attic.

The valet occupied a room at the very top of the turret. From his skylight window he overlooked the entire part of the park which extended from the gate to the steps of the front entrance.

This is the reason why Gustave Colinet was not asleep:

By an extraordinary stroke of luck, taking advantage of a short break in the clouds which occurred (as we recall) during the afternoon, the valet had gone for a short walk around the manor.

Hearing Verdinage coming in his direction, accompanied by Clodoche, dragging his crutch through the gravel, Gustave was about to beat a discreet retreat when a snippet of intriguing conversation reached his ears.

The servant's natural inquisitiveness caused him to hide discreetly behind a large stone urn, the better to listen.

Which is how he learnt about the mission the lord of the manor had entrusted to the cripple.

After his shift was finished, the valet went up to his room but, instead of going to bed, he sat down on a chair by the window, from which observation post he was perfectly positioned to see the strange visitor Clodoche had been ordered to bring to the manor.

He could clearly see the steps of the front entrance and the driveway as far as the circular fountain, thanks to the wet gravel which glistened in the moonlight. The rest of the driveway was lost in darkness.

A fine rain had obstinately started again. Sharp gusts of wind caused the weathervanes to squeak and the trees to groan.

The glacial damp of the night fell on Gustave's narrow shoulders and he shivered.

The valet was sensitive to the cold. He left the window and lay down on the bed, fully clothed.

Eyes wide open, Gustave wondered what fantastic being was about to arrive, led by the cripple. He vowed not to miss the spectacle.

....

On the ground floor, Thérèse reacted nervously to the slightest noise disturbing the tranquillity of the night.

Ever since her husband had found the second menacing letter, the housemaid-nanny had been counting the days.

She knew, just like everyone else at Marchenoire, that one month after the arrival of the second letter, a third and final warning, containing the owner's death warrant, would arrive at the manor.

Without revealing her thoughts—so as not to annoy Verdinage, who would fly off the handle at any mention of such phantasmagorias— she had been counting the days.

In addition, she had been struck by the haggard look of the young secretary, even though he had made every effort to hide his thoughts from the servants.

From that point, the housemaid had been convinced that the third letter had indeed arrived, and bad things were about to happen on that night of October 28.

Because her master didn't want anyone to appear concerned about the disturbing mystery, the housemaid-nanny respected his wishes and affected indifference, but nothing in this world would stop her from protecting her "little one" without his knowledge.

The good woman informed her husband of her decision. Charles, slightly tipsy, treated her like a madwoman. Nevertheless, the two of them agreed to take it in turns to keep watch from their room whilst everyone else was asleep.

Up until eleven o'clock, Thérèse, all ears, kept a conscientious watch.

All she could detect outside was the continuous pattering of the rain and the howling of the wind as it swirled around the chimneys.

Next to her, Charles was snoring with his mouth wide open.

Sensing that she would soon succumb, despite her desire to stay awake, the housemaid-nanny grabbed her husband by the arm and shook him awake.

'Huh? What? What's the matter?' he groaned, sitting up.

'Nothing, you old fool,' replied his wife gruffly. 'But I think I'm about to fall asleep and I want you to relieve me... Get dressed, lazybones!... Don't let me sleep for more than an hour! ... And wake me up immediately if ... the thing happens!'

Charles stretched and got dressed, still yawning.

....

The dogs were barking in their kennels....

Gustave was instantly on his feet. He ran to the skylight and looked straight down in the direction of the park gate.

It was pitch dark and a fine rain was falling incessantly.

There, at the very foot of the driveway, was a point of light surrounded by a red halo: Clodoche's lantern.

The mysterious visitor had arrived....

The valet never took his eyes off the zig-zagging light which was slowly getting bigger and clearer.

In addition to the sound of crunching gravel, another familiar sound reached Gustave Colinet's ears: Clodoche's crutch being dragged over the stones.

Little by little, two figures emerged from the darkness, one—which the servant recognised immediately—was Clodoche, who was carrying the lantern and walking slowly, forcing himself to illuminate the driveway in front of his badly-shod and malformed feet. The other person was following behind the cripple.

Colinet strained to see better: the figure behind Clodoche was walking with his head down, his hat jammed down on his head, and his coat collar up around his ears. It was impossible to see his face, and the lantern provided only a moving circle of light, which left his upper body in semi-darkness.

The visitor and his guide reached the front steps.

The valet, who had hoped to discern the features of the mysterious newcomer—even for just a moment—was disappointed: Clodoche had placed the lantern on the steps, following the instructions he had received.

He believed he could satisfy his curiosity another way. By slipping quietly out of his room and tip-toeing downstairs to the ground floor, he should be able to hide in one of the rooms close to the library, where the lord of the manor planned to meet the stranger.

Whilst Verdinage was accompanying the visitor from the front door to the library, he might be able to see the latter clearly in the well-lit entrance hall.

Just as he was cautiously opening his door, he heard the click of the front door being unlocked: Verdinage, lying in wait, must have opened it for his visitor before the latter had made an appearance.

Gustave Colinet was about to set foot silently on the landing when he heard voices below: the lord of the manor and the mystery man were beginning a conversation.

The sudden sound of a shot startled the servant. Then he heard an agonised cry....

Gustave Colinet stood dumbfounded for several seconds, paralysed by emotion. He pulled himself together and told himself that the mysterious stranger—whether he had shot at Verdinage or had himself been the target—would try to run away as quickly as possible, and that Clodoche would probably be powerless to stop him.

The valet had only one thought: to see the criminal's face!

Gustave Colinet hastily turned back and made a bee-line for the skylight.

Immediately after the shot had been fired in the entrance hall, there had been a deafening noise outside. His body half out of the skylight, Gustave Colinet could now see Clodoche standing on the last step, banging furiously on the front door with his crutch and shouting ominously.

The cripple clamped his hand on the door knob and tried turning it in all directions, but all his efforts were in vain.

At last the door, opened by someone on the inside, yielded to the cripple's attack.

The door shut again immediately afterwards. Only then did Gustave leave his observation post and dive towards the staircase.

When he reached the first landing, he leant over the banister and saw that Edmond Tasseau, taking the stairs four at a time, had almost reached the ground floor.

....

The barking of the dogs, which had alerted the valet, raised Thérèse from her slumber.

She looked around.

Charles was no longer in the room.

Her first thought was that her husband had gone out to find out what was disturbing the Great Danes.

She waited anxiously.

The alarm clock was showing half past one.

The housemaid-nanny strained her ears, but could only hear the pattering of the rain and the low moaning of the wind.

Despite her age, Thérèse had good hearing. She soon recognised a new sound, slight at first but becoming clearer: the crunching of gravel under someone's shoes. Somebody was walking in the park.

The noise of footsteps grew louder. As far as Thérèse could tell, the person approaching was not alone.

She could clearly discern the scraping of shoes, accompanied by a regular dull thud (she realised later it was the sound of Clodoche's crutch hitting the stone steps), followed by a metallic sound (Clodoche putting his lantern down).

The front door of the manor was opened.

At that moment, Verdinage and the stranger must have been face to face, because the master's voice—which Thérèse recognised clearly—exclaimed irritably:

'No! I won't leave!'

A shot rang out, followed by an agonised cry which faded into a groan.

Pinned to her bed, the housemaid collected her wits with difficulty. Making a determined effort, the courageous Thérèse got up and made her way to the entrance hall as quickly as possible.

Whilst still a few metres away, she could hear Clodoche shouting and pounding on the front door with his crutch.

Above her, doors were slamming. The servants were calling to one another noisily and starting to come downstairs.

Finally, the housemaid-nanny reached the hall.

The first thing she saw was her husband, paralysed by fear, *standing on the top step of the cellar stairs.*

Suddenly Charles got hold of himself, ran across the hall and opened the door to Clodoche, who hadn't stopped shouting and banging. The cripple almost toppled forward. The butler held him up with one hand and swiftly closed the door with the other, in an instinctive measure of security.

Breathing heavily, Edmond Tasseau appeared at the other end of the hall.

'What's going on?' asked the chauffeur, hurrying over to Charles.

Edmond and Charles, and, behind them, Clodoche and Thérèse, attempted to push on the half-open door of the library.

Gustave Colinet, making an appearance at the other end of the hall, saw them recoil in unison in horror and amazement.

He rushed forward just in time to catch the housemaid, who had fainted and was about to fall to the floor.

The valet stared.

The body of Napoléon Verdinage lay on the library floor, not far from where he was standing.

A bullet had entered his master's left eye and exited at the back of his head, causing his cranium to explode. A pool of blood was starting to spread, staining the carpet.

Edmond Tasseau stammered:

'The k-killer? ... W-where's the k-killer?'

There did not seem to be any possible hiding-place in the library. The chauffeur pulled back the curtains covering the windows, which were locked. As for the monumental stone fireplace, out of commission since the grocer had installed central heating at Marchenoire, it could not provide refuge either.

Followed by Clodoche, dragging his crutch, Edmond rapidly visited every room on the ground floor. Everywhere, the windows were closed and the iron shutters firmly secured.

The chauffeur hastened towards the staircase in order to explore the upper floors. Jeanne, the cook, was coming down unsteadily, clutching the banister with clenched hands.

'Did anyone come up?' asked the chauffeur anxiously.

His wife, unable to speak, shook her head.

'What about the cellar?' asked a calm voice.

They turned towards Gustave Colinet, who had just spoken. He was kneeling next to Thérèse, who was still lying inanimate on the floor of the entrance hall.

'The murderer is not in the cellar!' murmured the butler in a trembling voice.

'How do you know?' retorted Gustave. 'Nobody has checked yet.'

Charles wiped his pale, moist brow with the back of his hand. He mumbled distractedly:

'True enough.'

The butler staggered towards the open cellar door and started down the steps.

All eyes were on him when he returned.

Charles, with a great effort, announced:

'The cellar is empty!'

He bolted the door behind him, gave the lock a double turn, and placed the key in his pocket.

The servants looked at each other. Their stupefaction was obvious as they confronted the incomprehensible situation.

The murderer had not run away: he had disappeared.

Suddenly someone called out from outside. 'Open up! Open up!'

'Who's there?' shouted Charles Chapon.

'It's me,' replied the voice. 'Me, Bénard.'

VIII

Perplexed, Lieutenant Taupinois stroked his moustache with a nervous hand.

He was a strapping fellow, whose confident bearing and close-fitting uniform made the hearts of the young ladies of Compiègne flutter at the regional ball.

Lieutenant Taupinois firmly believed he possessed the talent of a Sherlock Holmes, and begrudged the secondary role that events had forced him to play. In the ten years he had served in the gendarmerie, his most notable exploits had been the mundane arrests of vagrants, chicken thieves, and uncooperative drunks.

One can only imagine the thrill that ran through his veins when, at one o'clock in the morning of the night of October 28 to October 29, a phone call notified him that a crime had been committed at Marchenoire Manor.

A crime! His lifelong dream! At last his name would appear in the newspapers, and, with any luck, his photograph as well. Journalists would be interviewing him.

For he had no doubt that the mere sight of his uniform would suffice to establish the truth and expose the criminal.

The inspectors of the flying squad would soon see that the gendarmerie was every bit as capable as they were of carrying out an important investigation.

He was going for the honour of the corps.

The lieutenant buckled his belt in a decisive manner and called Brigadier (2) Hémard and Gendarme Binet to accompany him.

The former was a tall, lanky fellow with a prominent nose. The latter, in contrast, was small, round and jovial with a habit of rolling his eyes.

Soon the three representatives of law and order were on horseback, galloping towards Compiègne.

(2) equivalent to Sergeant

They rode in the rain, carefully making their way in the black night. Trickles of water streamed down from the peaks of their soaked kepis. Fine droplets glistened on their moustaches.

'Bloody weather,' groused Brigadier Hémard.

Lost in thought, the lieutenant failed to hear him.

Gendarme Binet saluted his superior and replied:

'Brigadier, you're right!'

Taupinois urged his mount to go faster. His two subordinates followed suit, and the nocturnal ride continued gloomily and in silence.

Eventually, the iron-shod hooves of the horses struck the gravel of the Marchenoire driveway and Bénard, who was on the front steps acting as lookout, went into the mansion through the open door and shouted:

'The gendarmes! The gendarmes are here!'

Lieutenant Taupinois, followed by the sergeant and the gendarme, entered the hall majestically and gave the assembled servants a searching look.

With a trembling finger, Charles pointed to the corpse on the library floor.

The old butler began:

'Here's what happened—.'

'Be quiet!' interrupted the officer, conscious of his authority. 'You will only speak when asked.'

He approached the body and crouched down. After a long silence he declared:

'There are no burn traces, so the shot was not from point blank range. Therefore we are clearly not in the presence of a suicide.'

The sergeant admired the perceptiveness of his chief and said, stroking the black moustache of which he was justifiably proud:

'Indubitably, lieutenant, we are in the presence of a crime, and, what's more, a murder.'

'Besides,' observed the gendarme timidly, 'if the victim had killed himself, there would be a weapon close to hand, and there plainly isn't one.'

Taupinois, who was still crouching next to the body, shrugged and pulled a fully-loaded Browning from the victim's pocket.

'Lieutenant....' stammered the sergeant.

'That's enough!' ordered the senior officer, determined that an inferior should not lead the investigation.

He turned to Gustave Colinet.

'Does the manor have more than one exit?'

'No, monsieur,' replied the valet. 'It's a major fault in the construction. The manor only has one door leading to the outside.'

Taupinois turned to Binet:

'Go and guard the entrance to the building,' he said, 'and don't let anyone out without my express permission.'

The gendarme clicked his heels, saluted, turned around, and left.

The officer continued:

'I hope no one has touched anything inside the room of the crime?'

'Oh, no!' exclaimed Edmond Tasseau. 'Everyone knows that, in such circumstances, nothing must be touched.'

Taupinois left the library, locked the door behind him, and sat down at a table in the small salon.

He summoned each of the servants to come before him and appointed the sergeant to act as a clerk of the court.

The most difficult deposition was that of Clodoche.

The unfortunate cripple, terrified at the sight of the uniforms, had completely lost his head.

He was choking, unable to utter a word.

Realising that he was dealing with a half-wit, the lieutenant used patience. He managed to find soothing words to calm the cripple.

The latter eventually managed to tell what he knew:

'Voila!' he mumbled, '... Monsieur told Clodoche this afternoon... that Clodoche should go to the park gate at night and wait for the "someone."'

'Can anyone else confirm that?' interrupted Taupinois, looking at the other witnesses.

'I can,' replied the valet calmly. 'I happened to be in the park yesterday afternoon, hidden behind a stone urn, when Monsieur gave Clodoche those instructions. I can repeat, word for word, the conversation that I heard—entirely by accident!—because I would never allow myself to be indiscreet to the point of....'

'Enough!' The lieutenant cut him off and turned back to Clodoche.

'In the night,' continued the cripple, 'Clodoche gets up quietly...

61

and leaves by the window of the little guardhouse where he sleeps...
Clodoche leaves by the window so as not to wake M. Bénard...
Monsieur had asked Clodoche not to make any noise... Clodoche
waits a long time in the rain... He has the lighted lantern hidden under
his coat... Clodoche keeps waiting... But the "someone" has already
arrived and Clodoche hasn't heard him... Clodoche tells the
"someone" what Monsieur has told him to say... "Follow me to the
manor... Somebody is waiting for you"... The "someone" comes with
Clodoche as far as the front steps... Clodoche puts the lantern down
on the step. Monsieur immediately opens the door to the "someone"...
The door closes on the "someone" and Monsieur... Clodoche listens.
He hears Monsieur shouting angrily at the "someone"... And then...
And then ....'

The cripple gasped for breath.

Taupinois helped him to continue his deposition.

'... And then you heard a shot?'

Clodoche agreed in an expressionless voice:

'Yes, yes! Clodoche hears the "boom" ... and also a loud cry which
makes Clodoche afraid... But Clodoche knows he has to get closer if
he hears a noise... Clodoche tries to go in... But the "someone" has
shut the door... Clodoche can't open it from the outside... Clodoche
shouts very loudly and bangs a lot on the door with his crutch. After a
while M. Charles opens the door... and Clodoche sees, in Monsieur's
library... the good Monsieur... dead!'

The cripple shook his head slowly.

'Did you see the face of the person whom you led from the park
gate to the door of the manor?' asked the officer.

'Clodoche lifted up his lantern... but the "someone" hid his face in
the collar of his coat, like this.'

The cripple demonstrated, hiding the lower part of his face.

'The "someone's" hat was pulled down,' he added, pulling his own
beret down to his eyes.

'As you were going up the driveway, did you get a look at the
person you were guiding?'

'Clodoche shone the lantern in front of him, so as not to fall...
Clodoche always looks where he places his feet and his crutch.'

The officer wanted immediate confirmation of what he had been
told. The housemaid confirmed that, judging by the noises she had

heard, it was an accurate account of what had happened.

Gustave Colinet, who had been an eyewitness to part of the drama, declared:

'I can confirm the testimony of Mme. Thérèse Chapon, and Clodoche's account. Monsieur Lieutenant, from my window on the top floor, I saw the murderer arrive, led by the cripple. In the darkness, I was not able to see the criminal's features, either.

'The murder of the late Monsieur offers nothing clear before the moment the murderer disappeared, without any of us being able to say how—.'

'That's enough!' interrupted the lieutenant brutally. 'I didn't ask you to elaborate. Let justice take its course!'

He stroked his moustache with a conquering air, to signify to all present that he himself would be "justice."

Taupinois ordered Hémard to read the cripple's deposition out loud.

'Perfect!' he declared, after the sergeant had finished reading. 'It's a childishly simple matter. We know, thanks to Clodoche's deposition—confirmed at several points by Colinet (Gustave), the victim's valet—how the murderer got in. It only remains for us to determine how the latter left the site after perpetrating his crime. In short, the case can be summarised in a few words: *A man got in... How did he get out?'*

The lieutenant ordered the servants to remain in the small salon and began a meticulous search of the premises.

He expected to find the murderer's hiding place without difficulty. He was disappointed.

It was certainly true that there were a number of nooks and crannies, and even cupboards, where someone could have hidden and, *because the entrance door had been continuously guarded before the arrival of the gendarmes*, logic dictated that such a person should still be trapped inside the manor.

But Taupinois failed to unearth any trace of the criminal.

He examined the windows. They were all closed and protected by iron shutters which only opened from the inside.

The lieutenant looked next at the monumental stone fireplace and said, with a knowing air:

'It would not be surprising if this fireplace held the key to the puzzle, because it's been confirmed that the murderer did not leave by the door or any of the windows.'

The valet started to speak:

'But, Monsieur Lieutenant—.'

'Be quiet! ordered Taupinois brusquely.

He added, pointing to the hearth:

'Remove the plaque!'

Sergeant Hémard knelt down and, not without difficulty, removed the metal plate. A central heating system had been installed at the base of the chimney. The radiator and the pipes took up all the space: not even a kitten could have lodged there.

'Of course! Of course!' muttered the officer in disappointment and frustration. 'The murderer couldn't have hidden or escaped through here. We have to look elsewhere.'

Taupinois, who had expected an easy triumph, was becoming disenchanted. It was dawning on him that a policeman's life was not as simple as he'd assumed.

'What do you think, Hémard?' he asked nervously of his subordinate, who was following him step by step, like a dog.

'What I think,' replied the other, 'is that the whole business is very hard to explain, and extremely complicated as well.'

'In other words, you have no idea,' retorted Taupinois ungraciously.

'That's right, lieutenant,' replied the sergeant, not noticing his chief's irony.

The officer returned to the small salon, where the servants were anxiously awaiting the results of the search.

He considered the faces of Charles and Thérèse Chapon, Edmond and Jeanne Tasseau, Gustave Colinet, Jacques Bénard, and Clodoche.

'I shall notify my superiors,' he informed them. 'The gendarme who is on duty at the door will remain there until the arrival of the authorities. None of you should leave the premises or enter the library until further notice.'

It was nearly five o'clock in the morning. Taupinois and Hémard were getting ready to leave when Adhémar Dupont-Lesguyères arrived at the manor.

He recoiled in shock at the sight of a representative of the law standing at the front door.

'What do you want?' asked the gendarme suspiciously.

'But I'm... I'm coming inside,' replied the Adonis disconcertedly.

Binet called his superior officer.

'I'm the Marquis Adhémar Dupont-Lesguyères, secretary to M. Verdinage,' explained the new arrival to the advancing lieutenant.

'It's true!' confirmed Charles.

The young man went pale and stammered:

'B-But what's happened?... Someone tell me.'

'Our poor master!' sobbed Thérèse.

Taupinois, without replying, opened the door to the library. Adhémar recoiled at the sight of the body lying on the carpet.

'My God! My God!' he exclaimed as the horrible truth dawned on him.

He staggered and almost fainted.

The lieutenant closed the door on the tragic sight. He fired questions rapidly at the secretary.

'Where have you come from?'

'But... I....'

'Come on!... Reply!... Don't you live in the manor?'

'Yes... But tonight I had obtained permission from monsieur... from poor M. Verdinage.'

'Can anyone here confirm what you say?'

The servants remained silent.

The sergeant gave an incredulous little cough.

Taupinois had recovered his earlier self-importance. Stroking his moustache, he continued offhandedly:

'So, you live in the manor, yet—by the strangest coincidence—you just happen to be absent on the night of the crime. Did you often request permission for nocturnal visits?'

'No... That was the first time.'

'Wonderful! And can you tell me where you spent the night?'

'I... I went to the regional ball at the café *Ménard jeune.*'

'But the ball at the café *Ménard jeune* ends at one o'clock in the morning and it's now nearly five o'clock!' retorted the lieutenant, consulting his wristwatch.

He made a sign to the sergeant.

'Hémard!'

'Lieutenant!' replied the other, saluting smartly.

'Go immediately to the café *Ménard jeune*, wake the patron up, and check monsieur's claims.'

On hearing those words, Adhémar went as white as a sheet. His legs folded under him, and he collapsed into one of the chairs, holding his head in his hands.

Half an hour later, Hémard returned, out of breath.

'Lieutenant, ' he panted, 'someone answering the description of monsieur'—he pointed to Adhémar, who was listening intently, his features tense—'joined the ball at the café *Ménard jeune* yesterday evening, at approximately ten o'clock, and danced with several young ladies of the region.'

'There, you see,' interjected the Adonis.

'The individual in question,' continued the sergeant, 'left the ball shortly before midnight.'

'No! No!' protested Adhémar feebly.

'Where were you between midnight and five o'clock in the morning?' asked Taupinois coldly.

'I... I don't know... I was....'

The officer paid no intention to Adhémar's distracted response. He asked, addressing Clodoche:

'Did the stranger you led from the park gate to the manor resemble the individual seated on that chair? Try to remember.'

The Adonis gave the cripple an agonised look.

'Clodoche couldn't see,' replied the cripple, after a pause for reflection. 'Clodoche doesn't know.'

'Did the stranger talk to you on the way?' continued Taupinois insistently. 'Was his voice one you recognised?'

'The "someone" didn't speak to Clodoche,' replied the cripple, without hesitation.

The officer smiled triumphantly.

He sent Adhémar into the small salon and left the gendarme Binet to guard the door, with instructions not to let the young secretary out of his sight until the arrival of the flying squad.

He rubbed his hands as he went back into the entrance hall.

'There's no doubt about it!' he declared, giving Brigadier Hémard a friendly pat on the shoulder, 'no doubt at all. We have the culprit!... Dupont-Lesguyères cannot account for his movements during the period when the crime was committed... When I questioned him on that precise point, he became agitated... That's indisputable proof of his guilt!'

66

'It's clear, lieutenant,' replied his subordinate, 'it's clear that the individual in question displayed manifest signs of guilt and, what's more, in an ostensible manner.'

As Taupinois happened to be close to a mirror, he drew himself up to his full height and contemplated his reflection with satisfaction.

He had realised the dream he had pursued for the last ten years:

He had solved a criminal case!

SECOND PART

A LABORIOUS INVESTIGATION

I

Whilst the criminal records office photographed the crime scene, looked for clues to the identity of the murderer, and took the fingerprints of all the occupants of the manor, Paul Malicorne (substitut du Procureur de la République (3)), Claude Launay (juge d'instruction (4)), and André Pruvost (commissaire divisionnaire de la brigade mobile (5)) were in lively discussion the large salon, under the watchful eye of clerk of the court, Ernest.

M. Launay was a young and energetic examining magistrate, determined to make a name for himself.

He had a bilious complexion, an angular face, and an imprecise hair parting. His wrinkled trousers overhung his shoes, and his scrawny body was loosely encased in a badly-fitting suit, but the examining magistrate paid little heed to such sartorial considerations.

Passionate about his work, and possessing real investigatory gifts, he would have obtained a well-deserved promotion, but for an extreme spirit of contradiction.

This curious flaw had caused him to commit serious blunders on several occasions.

A police detective merely had to hint at a theory for M. Launay, without even the pretence of an examination, to offer a diametrically opposed one, even one which defied elementary common sense.

One can imagine how many times such an attitude had harmed an investigation.

Those familiar with this trait knew how to compensate for it by never taking a precise position, but simply hinting at it.

(3) deputy state prosecutor   (4) examining magistrate (5) flying squad superintendent

69

Sometimes they even took a position contrary to their true belief, in order for him to support the outcome they desired.

The first act of M. Launay, upon his arrival at Marchenoire, was to release Adhémar Dupont-Lesguyères, suspected by Lieutenant Taupinois.

André Pruvost, the flying squad superintendent, provided the magistrate with highly unfavourable information about the secretary:

'Adhémar Dupont-Lesguyères appears a strong suspect from several points of view,' he said. 'He's a young man with a far from brilliant past, who escaped prison by the skin of his teeth for writing a cheque which bounced. Let's not forget too quickly that, before becoming Napoléon Verdinage's private secretary, this young tearaway gave himself over to debauchery, showing no moral compass. In a word, the Marquis Adhémar Dupont-Lesguyères is depraved!'

'Depraved is a strong word,' thundered M. Launay. 'Whilst I admit that this young man had dubious connections and almost went to jail, those are merely the peccadilloes of the son of a noble family. Until I have more concrete information to the contrary, I shall consider Adhémar Dupont-Lesguyères to be innocent of Verdinage's murder.'

He accompanied that declaration with disparaging remarks aimed at gendarmes "who think they are policemen, but who serve no other purpose than to send investigations on the wrong track, so as to complicate the simplest situations."

The secretary, now free, thanked the magistrate effusively for his decision and offered to provide him with any information that he might require.

M. Launay deigned to give a nod of agreement, then proceeded to pull Lieutenant Taupinois's report out of his pocket, roll it up, set fire to it, and use it to light a cigar stub, which emitted a disagreeable smell.

The fat, self-important deputy state prosecutor wiped his gold-rimmed spectacles, stroked his blonde beard at length, and emitted a groan which could equally well have been a sign of agreement or of protest.

Truth be told, M. Malicorne was indecisive and displeased. He

70

hated complications and suspected that the present matter would take a long time to solve.

He had already been involved in another such case, two years earlier: the mysterious death of M. Desrousseaux.

M. Desrousseaux (lest we forget) was the unfortunate owner who had purchased Marchenoire Manor following the death of the banker Abraham Goldenberg. He was found lying in the park one evening, dead from a rifle shot. The top detectives from Compiègne and Paris had led the investigation. It was known that M. Desrousseaux had received three threatening letters ordering him to leave *the forbidden house*. The anonymous writer of those letters was never found. The matter was eventually closed.

The deputy had a bad memory of that experience, and it was without enthusiasm that he found himself involved with a similar tragedy. He anticipated that the current investigation, like the last, would end in failure.

Distant and cynical, he participated in the routine investigations without hope or enthusiasm.

M. Launay invited Adhémar Dupont-Lesguyères, whom he considered a cut above the other servants, to sit next to him.

The Adonis, charmed by the special attention he was receiving, had regained his composure and self-assurance.

The magistrate consulted a handwritten list and ordered the gendarme on duty to bring in Bénard, who came forward hesitantly with an anxious and evasive look.

M. Launay interrogated him in a decidedly unfriendly manner:

'Name?'

'Bénard... Jacques Bénard.'

'Profession?'

'Guard... and gardener on occasion.'

'How long have you been in M. Verdinage's service?'

'Since he purchased the manor, monsieur le juge. Three months, more or less.'

Adhémar intervened:

'Monsieur le juge d'instruction,' he explained, 'Bénard worked for the first owner. He was previously in the employ of Abraham Goldenberg....'

'The famous crook?'

'The very same... and then in the employ of M. Desrousseaux, and then....'

'That's right!' exclaimed the deputy suddenly, smacking his forehead. 'I remember being present at this man's previous interrogation during the Desrousseaux affair.'

M. Launay looked the guard up and down, whilst the latter twisted his cap nervously in his hands.

'What do you think about the crime?' continued the magistrate.

'Absolutely nothing.'

'Come, come! You must have an opinion.'

'About that, no. I don't know anything. I went to bed at nine o'clock and slept so soundly I didn't even hear Clodoche—.'

'Clodoche is an unfortunate cripple whom Bénard recruited out of charity.'

'I know!' said M. Launay curtly. 'The gendarme lieutenant told me about his role in the affair. I'll summon Clodoche in good time. Continue, Bénard.'

'As I was saying, monsieur le juge, I was sleeping so soundly that I didn't hear Clodoche get up to go and wait at the park gate for the stranger that M. Verdinage was expecting.'

'You're a heavy sleeper, for a guard!' observed deputy Malicorne.

M. Launay shot an irritated glance at the interrupter and continued:

'You were sleeping, Bénard, yet you managed to appear at the front door of the manor, dressed from head to foot, fifteen minutes after the discovery of the body by Verdinage's servants.'

'I was awakened by a shot, and got dressed as quickly as I could, and ran... too late, because the crime had already been committed and the murderer had disappeared.'

The deputy turned on Bénard, and interrupted again:

'You managed to hear a shot from inside the manor, at least twenty metres from your lodgings, yet you failed to notice the dogs barking in the kennel right next door to your room. You have very peculiar hearing!'

'But....'

'Because it seems that the dogs started barking as soon as the stranger appeared at the park gate.'

Bénard hesitated for a moment, then stammered:

'It's true, monsieur le substitut.'

'Well, well! So you did hear them?'

'I heard them, monsieur le substitut, but I didn't think anything of it because those damned animals bark for nothing. I simply assumed a villager had walked near the gates and I went back to sleep.'

M. Launay lit a second cigar, just as foul-smelling as the first, using the smouldering stub. He continued:

'You were asleep... a detonation woke you up. You got dressed. You ran to the manor... Very well!... At that moment, was the entrance door open or shut?'

'It was shut, and there was a lantern shining on the top step.'

'As you were running towards the manor, did you pass anyone running away?'

'No, monsieur le juge, for I would have arrested anyone found on the property.'

'Very well!... So someone opened the door... You went in... Was the door closed behind you *immediately*?'

'Yes, monsieur le juge, *immediately*. And it remained shut for the whole time we searched the manor to try and find the murderer. I was the one who eventually opened it, and I sat on the steps to await the arrival of the gendarmes.'

'In short, according to you, *it's absolutely impossible for the murderer, once inside the manor, to have escaped by using the same route he used to enter, but in the opposite direction?*'

'That's my opinion, monsieur le juge.'

'Do you know anyone who would have an interest in making your master disappear?'

'Yes, monsieur le juge.'

M. Malicorne gave a start:

'Who?' he asked, in a voice trembling with emotion.

'The person who wrote the anonymous letters,' replied Bénard.

The deputy balked at the idea:

'I've read the letters. They're idiotic! There's no proof that there's the slightest connection between them and Verdinage's murder.'

'Nevertheless, monsieur le substitut....'

M. Launay intervened:

'That's enough!... You're here as a witness, nothing more... I ask you to confine yourself to answering the questions, not to substitute for me by advancing your own suppositions, well founded or not.

Please sign your deposition and leave. I'll call you if I have any further questions.'

M. Malicorne turned to the examining magistrate and screeched, his arms raised to the ceiling:

'They're all the same!... If we let them all talk, we'll be in a fine mess... How can you expect people like that to solve such a mysterious crime when we, professional investigators, are still not sure?... at least about certain details....'

II

Edmond Tasseau followed Bénard before the examining magistrate.

'Your name is Tasseau (Edmond). You are the victim's chauffeur, are you not?'

'Yes, monsieur le juge.'

'Since when?'

'It's been four years, monsieur le juge.'

'Did you have any reason to complain about your master?'

'No, monsieur le juge. M. Verdinage was the best of masters, as long as he was served honestly and conscientiously.'

'Were you aware that the victim had received a third threatening letter?'

'No, monsieur le juge. In order to hide the fact from all the servants, M. Verdinage preferred to use the services of Clodoche, rather than ask one of us; me, for example.'

'At what time did you go to bed on the night of October 28?'

'At the same time as my wife, at half past ten.'

'What woke you up?'

'A shot. I also heard a cry of agony at the same time. I put my trousers on and hurried downstairs.'

'What did you see when you reached the hall?'

'I saw M. Charles, Mme. Thérèse, and Clodoche, for whom the butler had just opened the front door. I went over to them. We saw our poor master lying on the library floor in a pool of blood.'

'Thank you,' replied M. Launay. 'Please ask your wife to come in.'

After the chauffeur had left, the magistrate observed to Dupont-Lesguyères:

'That witness is a fine figure of an honest man!'

'We were all devoted to our master,' replied the secretary.

Jeanne appeared, still visibly shaken.

'Don't worry, madame,' said the magistrate, pointing to a chair.

Jeanne slumped down and waited anxiously to be questioned.

'Jeanne Tasseau, how long have you been M.Verdinage's cook?' asked M. Launay.

'M-My husband and I were hired together, four years ago,' stammered the cook.

'At what time did you go to bed?'

'At half past ten, after our service had finished . I was woken by a shot, and so was my husband. There was a terrible cry... I'll never forget it... Edmond rushed out of the room, half-dressed... I was horribly afraid... I heard shouting and banging at the front door... I found out later that it was Clodoche asking to be let in... I put on a dressing gown and went downstairs as best as I could, clutching the banister... I kept thinking I was going to be sick and never make it all the way down.'

'What were the other servants doing when you got to the bottom of the stairs?'

'My husband and Clodoche had just checked all the rooms on the ground floor. Gustave was helping M. Charles to treat Mme. Thérèse, who was lying unconscious in front of the library door.'

'Needless to say, *if the murderer had tried to take refuge on the first or second floor, you would have met him on the staircase?*'

'There's no doubt about it, monsieur le juge. Particularly since Edmond had already switched the lights on as he went down.'

'Your deposition is clear and precise, Madame Tasseau. Please sign this paper... Thank you!... Please call the valet... Let me see. What's his name?'

The magistrate consulted his list.

'Gustave Colinet, monsieur le juge,' said Adhémar.

Jeanne left the room.

The valet came in, bowed silently, and waited impassively.

M. Launay looked at him for a moment and then asked:

'Have you been in the victim's employ for a long time?'

'For three years and two months, monsieur le juge. Since I left college. This is my first job.'

'You graduated from college?' said the magistrate in astonishment.

'Yes, monsieur le juge. I hold a baccalaureate. I failed my law licence.'

'And now you're a valet?'

'My father is dead, ruined by bad investments. I wasn't able to continue my studies. I had to live. Besides, M. Verdinage was a benevolent employer.'

'Let's get back to the night of the crime,' said M. Launay brusquely. 'At what time did you go up to your room?'

'At the same time as Jeanne and Edmond. At about ten thirty, monsieur le juge.'

'Did you go to sleep straight away?'

'No, monsieur le juge. As I already told monsieur the lieutenant of the gendarmerie, I had overheard—quite by accident, monsieur le juge!—the instructions our late master had given Clodoche. Intrigued and anxious, I decided to watch from my window, from where I could see all of that part of the park which extends in front of the manor. But the cold forced me to stop. I lay down on my bed.'

'Did you hear the dogs bark?'

'Yes, monsieur le juge. I went quickly over to the skylight. Shortly afterwards I saw Clodoche, with a lantern in his hand, coming towards the house, accompanied by a stranger whose features I was unable to discern. They climbed the front steps. Out of curiosity, I opened the door of my room. .. I thought I could hear voices in the hall... Suddenly there was a shot, followed by Monsieur's heart-rending cry... Then I went back to the skylight.'

'You say that, from there, you can see all of that part of the park which extends in front of the manor. Therefore, if someone had escaped through the front door, you would have seen them, would you not?'

'Assuredly, monsieur le juge. Despite the darkness, I could clearly distinguish the driveway, down as far as the fountain. In addition, Clodoche's lantern lit up the top of the steps. I only saw the cripple banging on the door with his crutch and shouting for someone to let him in to see his master.'

'And when did you leave the window?'

'After someone opened the door for Clodoche and he disappeared inside.'

'And was the door closed behind the cripple?'

'Immediately behind him, monsieur le juge.'

'And then you went downstairs to the ground floor?'

'Yes, monsieur le juge, and I arrived just in time to catch Mme. Thérèse in my arms as she fainted at the sight of Monsieur's body.'

'And then you knelt beside her, next to her husband, whilst Edmond Tasseau, followed by Clodoche, searched the rooms on the ground floor?'

'Yes, monsieur le juge; M. Charles only left us to visit the cellar, the only place that hadn't been searched.'

'Ah! So it was M. Charles who visited the cellar?'

'He's the butler, Charles Chapon,' explained Adhémar.

Le magistrate made a gesture of annoyance at the interruption, and continued:

'And Charles Chapon didn't notice anything suspicious in the cellar?'

'No, monsieur le juge. And there wasn't anyone down there, either.'

'So, for the entire time that Edmond Tasseau and Clodoche were searching the ground floor, you were stationed in front of the library door?'

'Yes, monsieur le juge.'

'Consequently, no one could have left the house of the crime?'

'No, monsieur le juge. *At least, not through the front door, which is very close to the door of the library.'*

'What did you do whilst you were waiting for the gendarmes to arrive?'

'Edmond helped M. Charles to carry Mme. Thérèse to her room, whilst Bénard phoned for the police from the office. As for me, I stayed by our master's body until the gendarmes arrived.'

'After he'd put his wife to bed, what did the butler do?'

'He remained by his poor wife's side. Edmond, Jeanne, and Clodoche went into the kitchen for some hot coffee.'

'Meanwhile, Bénard opened the front door and sat outside on the steps, I believe?'

'Yes, monsieur le juge. I could see him very clearly from where I was, inside the library. The door to the hallway was open. I was only a few metres away from the guard.'

M. Launay got up and paced up and down the salon.

Gustave Colinet exited discreetly, after having signed the clerk of the court's register.

'To sum up,' said deputy prosecutor Malicorne, stroking his beard, 'to sum up, the problem is clear-cut: the murderer entered the manor, committed his crime, and disappeared without trace.'

The magistrate stopped pacing the room and agreed:

'There you have it. It's perfectly simple. Put like that, the problem before us is crystal clear.'

The superintendent, silent up to that point, scratched his head and observed:

'What's unfortunate is that we don't know *how* the murderer disappeared.'

'Thank you for that,' retorted M. Launay.

The deputy, who was out of ideas, did not know what to say and so pretended to be deep in thought.

The magistrate took the depositions of Bénard, Edmond, Jeanne, and Gustave out of the clerk's hands. He read them attentively, underlining the passages he found particularly interesting with a fingernail.

'Everything is of a marvellous precision,' he murmured. 'The declarations of the various witnesses agree exactly.'

He rubbed his hands in satisfaction and declared:

'I'm beginning to see the light.'

The deputy looked at him quizzically.

The superintendent opened his mouth to speak.

'I'm beginning to see the light,' repeated the magistrate forcefully.

He called out to the gendarme on duty at the door:

'Bring in Mme. Thérèse Chapon.'

The tone in which the order was given led the deputy and the superintendent, without understanding why, to believe that the investigation had just taken a decisive step forward.

III

The housemaid-nanny entered.

Dragging her leg, she moved slowly and appeared worn out. She was no longer the dominant wife, used to upbraiding her husband sharply, but an old woman with a sad face and a back bent with pain.

The examining magistrate, possibly moved by the unfortunate woman's pitiful appearance, welcomed her deferentially and invited her to sit down. Thérèse obeyed, automatically and unthinkingly. Suddenly she burst into tears. For several minutes, she sobbed convulsively. Little by little she calmed down. Silent tears rolled down her cheeks and onto her clasped hands.

She moaned feebly:

'My poor Napo... my little one.'

'Mme. Thérèse Chapon was M. Verdinage's wet nurse,' explained Adhémar Dupont-Lesguyères. 'Our late master loved her dearly. She acted as the steward of the manor.'

M. Launay waited until the housemaid-nanny had recovered her spirits somewhat, then began to question her in a gentle and kindly manner:

'At what time did you go to bed on the night of October 28?'

'I... I... don't know... I...'

'At ten thirty, I presume, at the same time as the other servants?'

'A little bit later, monsieur le juge. I'm in the habit of making a tour of the premises after all the others have gone to their rooms, to make sure that all the doors and windows are properly shut.'

'And, on the night of the crime, did you perform your duty with the same thoroughness as the other nights?'

'Oh, yes, monsieur le juge.'

'Windows and doors were properly shut?'

'Yes, monsieur le juge. The iron shutters were shut everywhere and properly locked.'

'Did you notice anything unusual?'

'Nothing, monsieur le juge.'

'Nevertheless, one door was unlocked: the door to the cellar.'

The housemaid-nanny hesitated visibly. Realising that the poor woman was not in full possession of her faculties, the magistrate continued firmly, but not brutally:

'Do you remember? ... Was the door to the cellar locked or unlocked?'

Thérèse eventually replied, but not confidently:

'I... I... think it was unlocked.'

'And who possesses the key to that door?'

'Charles, my husband.'

M. Launay did not dwell on the point, but continued:

'If a stranger to the mansion had been hidden in one of the rooms of the ground floor prior to the crime, would you have discovered him on your rounds?'

'Oh, yes!... When I do my rounds I look everywhere, I open the cupboards, and I stick a broom under the furniture.'

The magistrate repeated:

'So there were no strangers in the manor that night?'

'None!'

'That is what I wanted to know.'

The magistrate played with his pencil for a moment, then looked out of the window and asked casually:

'After you finished your daily rounds and went back to your ground floor room, what was your husband doing?'

'He was already sleeping like a log. I didn't try to wake him, as I preferred to keep watch myself.'

'What watch?'

'I believe I explained already, monsieur le juge,' interceded Adhémar Dupont-Lesguyères. 'Mme. Thérèse and her husband had decided to keep watch all night long, taking turns.'

'So were you expecting something to happen?' asked M. Launay, addressing Thérèse.

'Ah, monsieur le juge, everyone knew how and when it would happen... The last letter was due to arrive one month after the second. When Charles found it on the cellar steps, I wrote the date down in my diary. That was September 28, which meant that the deadline would be October 28. I saw from the dismay on M. Dupont-Lesguyères's face on that date that I wasn't mistaken and that my master had received the sinister message.'

82

'I confess, monsieur le juge,' conceded Adhémar, 'that I became very anxious when I opened the envelope whilst accompanying M. Verdinage in the car.'

'Then it's regrettable that you didn't contact the police,' replied the magistrate reproachfully. 'A tragic event could have been avoided.'

'M. Verdinage would not allow me to,' responded the secretary. 'He didn't even want the servants to know about the third letter. He treated the letters as if they were the work of a prankster with bad taste. Not wanting to upset the servants, he made me promise to keep silent. Unfortunately, I was unable to hide my anxiety from Mme. Thérèse.'

'Let us continue, Madame,' said M. Launay, cutting him off and turning back to Thérèse. 'Having observed nothing out of the ordinary on your rounds, you returned to your room and found your husband asleep. Then what?'

'Feeling tired, I shook Charles, who got dressed. I told him to remain alert and to wake me up at the slightest sign of trouble. After that, I went to bed... I was woken up by the dogs barking.'

'So it wasn't your husband who woke you?' asked the magistrate.

The housemaid-nanny blushed and stammered. Finally, pressed to express herself clearly, she admitted:

'When the yapping of the Great Danes woke me up, *Charles was no longer in the room.*'

M. Launay smiled and shot a knowing glance at the deputy.

He lit a cigar and continued his questioning:

'Didn't your husband's absence surprise you?'

'I thought he'd gone to look at what was happening outside.'

'What time would that have been?'

'I don't... No, wait... I remember looking at the alarm clock: it was half past one.'

'Which puts it at approximately the time of the crime. Please continue. You presumably got up?'

'Not straight away. I was still waiting for Charles to come and tell me what was happening. I didn't hear anything for several minutes, then there was the sound of footsteps on the gravel... Someone was approaching the house.'

'I see. And then?'

'I heard someone climb the steps to the front door... I distinctly heard the sound of a cane on the stone.'

'That would be Clodoche's crutch,' said M. Launay, pleased with his own perspicacity.

'After that, I heard a slight metallic sound.'

'That would be Clodoche's lantern as he set it down,' observed the magistrate smugly.

'I heard the front door open... I heard Monsieur speaking. He seemed angry. He was saying: "No! I won't leave!"'

'Did you recognise the voice of the one speaking?'

'Yes. It was definitely Napo... M. Verdinage.'

'And then?'

'Suddenly there was a terrible detonation... and... I heard the cry... the heart-rending cry of my poor little one as he was shot to death.'

The housemaid-nanny collapsed in a new crisis of despair.

The magistrate, clearly irritated, shrugged his shoulders and continued brusquely:

'Was your husband also out of the room when this happened?'

'Yes, Monsieur,' replied Thérèse, after a slight hesitation which did not escape the notice of the magistrate, the deputy, or the superintendent.

'Did you not think that, when M. Verdinage used the words "No! I won't leave!" he might have been talking to your husband?'

'I... I thought so at first, but the shot proved to me that it wasn't Charles who was with our master in the library.'

M. Launay sank further into the armchair, crossed his legs, and announced solemnly:

'Madame Chapon, I'm going to ask you a vitally important question, to which I want you to respond unequivocally.'

'I'm all ears, monsieur.'

The magistrate paused, then looked the housemaid-nanny straight in the eye as he asked:

'Where was Charles, your husband, after you dressed, left your room, and descended into the hall?'

Thérèse, wild-eyed, babbled a few indistinct words.

M. Launay relentlessly repeated the question, his eyes never leaving the housemaid's face.

Visibly trembling, she gasped:

'Charles was coming out of the cellar... He was on the first step.'

'You're lying!' declared the magistrate.

'Oh, monsieur!' said the maid, her face purple with indignation.

The magistrate continued forcefully:

'I demand the truth, the whole truth.'

'But....'

'The witness Edmond Tasseau, who reached the hall after you did, affirms that he saw your husband *near the door to the library.*'

'Yes, monsieur, that's true, because my husband ran towards the front door when he heard Clodoche banging and shouting for someone to open, because, without a key, the lock only opens from the inside.'

'You maintain that, when you arrived, Charles Chapon was *on the first cellar step, which is at the other end of the hall from the library?*'

'I swear it, monsieur.'

'Thank you,' concluded M. Launay. 'Sign your deposition and tell your husband I'm ready for him.'

As Thérèse was leaving, a man in white came in. It was Docteur Pierre, the celebrated medical examiner. His face, which sported a walrus moustache, was beaming and jovial.

He shook hands with the three representatives of justice and said:

'I've just completed my examination of Verdinage... The results are conclusive. He was killed with an eight millimetre bullet from a regulation revolver. It entered between the nose and the left eye, exited at the back of the head and was half embedded in the wall... The victim was three-quarters turned towards his killer... The crime was committed at half past one... The bullet was fired from a distance of five metres... The murderer was practically in the doorway to the library when he pulled the trigger.'

'Perfect, Docteur!' exclaimed the magistrate. 'We couldn't have hoped for more precision.'

The medical examiner bowed and left in the company of the superintendent.

M. Launay rubbed his hands and said to the deputy:

'What do you think, M. Malicorne?'

The other extinguished his cigar and declared:

'Now we are in possession of all the facts in the case, the solution is close to hand.... What am I saying?... We have it!'

IV

The butler came forward and stopped a few steps away from the magistrate.

He was as white as a sheet and shivered continuously.

He replied to the first few questions in a clipped voice:

'I've been in M. Verdinage's service since my marriage to Thérèse, that is to say for twelve years.'

'You are, consequently, an old servant in whom M. Verdinage could have absolute confidence.'

'Monsieur Verdinage would not have kept a servant in whom he did not have absolute trust,' interjected Adhémar Dupont-Lesguyères.

'And did Charles Chapon enjoy the full confidence of his master?' asked M. Launay.

'Absolute confidence,' replied the secretary categorically.

The magistrate turned to the butler:

'For your part, Charles Chapon, I won't ask you if you were attached to your master.'

'I would have been a monster of ingratitude otherwise,' replied the other.

Once again, Adhémar Dupont-Lesguyères interceded:

'My responsibilities as private secretary,' he said self-importantly, 'mean that I am privy to the details of the deceased's will. I know that Charles Chapon, together with his wife, are the principal beneficiaries. M. Verdinage was more or less without a family, his only relatives being distant cousins.'

The young secretary's declaration seemed of great interest to M. Launay, who asked the butler:

'Were you aware of what M. Verdinage had left you in his will?'

'Er, well, monsieur le juge,' replied the servant evasively. 'I... I...I did think he might... but....'

'What?' said the secretary in astonishment. 'You knew perfectly well that M. Verdinage had left you a considerable sum. Do I need to remind you that, several days before the tragic event, you....'

The Adonis bit his tongue, realising that his remarks were putting the butler in jeopardy.

The magistrate, intrigued, ordered him to explain himself.

'It's just a detail,' murmured the secretary, 'a detail of no importance. I reminded Charles in passing because he indicated....'

'Who indicated what?' asked M. Launay.

'Monsieur le juge, during a severe reprimand concerning his intemperance, M. Verdinage threatened to cut Charles out of his will if he didn't mend his ways.'

The magistrate turned to Charles.

'And so, you knew you were the principal heir to M. Verdinage's estate?'

The butler attempted to respond, but M. Launay would not give him time:

'Let's move on!' he said with a sneer. 'Tell me exactly *where you were* when the crime was being committed, because, according to your wife, you had left your room.'

'Where I was?'

The butler wiped his brow with the sleeve of his jacket.

He made a supreme effort and articulated with difficulty:

'I... I was... I was making my rounds.'

'Your rounds? Where? In the manor? In the park?'

'In... in the park.'

'So therefore, you must have heard the dogs barking. Didn't that make you nervous?'

'I didn't hear anything.'

'Not even footsteps on the gravel?'

'No, monsieur le juge.'

'But, good heavens, Gustave Colinet, from his room on the top floor, and your wife on the ground floor, clearly heard those various noises. It's not possible that you, *and you alone*, heard nothing.'

Charles Chapon remained silent.

'Do you understand,' continued the magistrate, 'what your silence allows me to infer? I haven't forgotten that it was *you* who supposedly discovered the second threatening letter on the steps down to the cellar *to which only you had a key*.'

'Monsieur le juge....'

'Nor have I forgotten that *you* are the principal beneficiary in the victim's will... and that you were recently threatened with the loss of a considerable fortune.'

'Monsieur le juge....'

Charles understood that the terrible finger of suspicion was pointing to him. He fought back:

'How could you imagine such an infamy, monsieur le juge?'

'I'm not imagining anything,' M. Launay snapped back.

'Nevertheless, you're accusing me....'

'I'm not accusing you of anything. I'm simply noting that your attitude is peculiar, to say the least, and I understand why your wife—who is an honest woman—was so reluctant in her testimony.'

The butler appeared to make a decision.

'I can see, monsieur le juge, that I have no way to vindicate myself other than to make a confession that will cost me dearly.'

'I'm listening.'

'I broke my word and shamefully let my master be killed.'

Adhémar Dupont-Lesguyères looked at the butler in astonishment, wondering whether the other had suddenly lost his mind.

Charles was accusing himself of being an accomplice?'

A triumphant gleam appeared in the magistrate's eye.

'Explain yourself!' he said. 'Justice will be grateful for your sincerity.'

'I promised monsieur that I wouldn't drink any more,' said the old servant, hanging his head in shame. I kept my word for a while... I really made an effort, I swear to you, monsieur le juge... But in the end it was stronger than I was and I returned to my vice. I'm the only one who has the key to the cellar, as a function of my duties... For several nights I went down to the cellar whilst everyone else was asleep... On the night of the crime....'

'On the night of the crime?' repeated M Launay, hanging on the butler's every word.

'On the night of the crime, after Thérèse woke me up, I promised myself I would not take a drink and would wait for the events to unfold.... But the temptation was too strong... I felt the key, which was tucked in my jacket pocket. Everything was calm, and I thought Thérèse's fears were exaggerated... My good woman was sound asleep as I tiptoed out of our room. I negotiated the main staircase silently, opened the door to the cellar, and went down.'

'How long were you down there?' asked the magistrate.

'I don't know, monsieur le juge... Suddenly I heard someone walking in front of the entrance door. I heard the door open... I was about to go up when I heard Monsieur's voice saying: "No! I won't leave!" It was not the moment to announce my presence in the cellar. What would Monsieur have said if he'd seen me come out at such an hour?... I was afraid of incurring his wrath, particularly since he already sounded furious. So....'

Charles Chapon stopped, choked by emotion.

'So,' he stammered, 'I heard a shot... I'm not brave, monsieur le juge. My whole body was shaking... If only the other servants had been there! I heard Monsieur groan, but I was frozen in place by fear. It was only when I heard Clodoche shouting from outside that I left the cellar and went up the steps as quickly as my unsteady legs would allow.'

'And that's when you ran into your wife?'

'Yes, monsieur le juge... she was coming out of our room just as I was coming out of the cellar... I was ashamed of what I had done... When Thérèse came to, after her fainting spell, I confessed everything, taking advantage of the fact that we were alone. I begged her not to reveal where she'd seen me emerging from. That's why she'd hesitated so much before speaking.'

Charles Chapon tugged at his moustache and wiped his face, which was covered in sweat.

'Continue!' ordered M. Launay.

'As I was saying, monsieur le juge, when I heard Clodoche's cries I took courage again. Clodoche is quite strong. I told myself he could lend a hand against the killer... I ran across the hall, opened the door to let Clodoche in, and closed the door after him... Edmond and Gustave arrived shortly afterwards. Edmond and Clodoche searched all the ground floor rooms without finding anything. Jeanne came down last.'

'Your account agrees well with those of your colleagues,' commented the magistrate, adding with a sceptical smile: 'Very well... almost too well!'

'Nevertheless—.'

'But why did you forget to tell me about the cellar?' cut in M. Launay. 'You're the one who visited it, after all.'

'I volunteered to visit and I visited it alone, because....'

'Because?'

'Because I knew there was no one down there, monsieur le juge. And I didn't want to draw the other servants' attention to the unlocked door. They'd seen me lock it last night, after dinner. I would have to have admitted to my guilty intemperance.'

'When the valet Gustave proposed that you both visit the cellar, you immediately replied: "He's not in the cellar."'

'I realised straight away that I'd made a stupid mistake.'

'Yet you did go down into the cellar again.'

'Yes, monsieur le juge. It was just for show, because *nobody could have hidden there, given that I'd been down there myself whilst the crime was happening, and afterwards there was always someone in the hall.* When I came back up, I automatically locked and bolted the door, without really knowing why.'

The butler burst into tears.

'I'm a miserable wretch, monsieur le juge! If I hadn't lapsed into my vice, I would have been in my room, at my post... But I'm a miserable coward, because I should have come up from the cellar right away... I would have seen my poor master's killer. I would have risked my life to stop him before he disappeared... disappeared who knows how?'

'Justice is close to finding out, Chapon,' replied the magistrate sternly. Please sign your deposition. I shall no doubt need you again, once certain details are cleared up.'

The butler took a step backwards.

'Not that way!' M. Launay told him. 'I don't want you communicating with the other servants, so please go through the small salon. An inspector will accompany you.'

Charles choked.

'You're arresting me!' he stammered.

'No. No,' protested the magistrate.

And he added, under his breath:

'Not yet!'

V

M. Launay was beaming. He offered his cigar case to the deputy, who made a show of refusing.

'That's right, I was forgetting. You only smoke luxury cigars. What do you expect, Monsieur Malicorne, I have disgusting taste. It comes from mixing with too many scoundrels. It's my profession that causes it.'

He got up, stretched, and continued:

'Come, now. It's not going too badly. That Charles Chapon is more wily than I suspected. We'll see how long he persists in his line of defence.'

'Huh?' grunted the deputy. 'You think that Charles Chapon...?'

'I'm not thinking anything. I have no imagination. Imagination is a very bad thing when you're conducting an investigation. One thing must have struck you, however, just as it struck me: the butler's attitude. Highly suspicious, to tell the truth. Highly suspicious!'

'He's a good man with an inoffensive manner. Besides which, he's been in Verdinage's service for twelve years.'

That was all that was needed to infuriate the volatile examining magistrate.

'What does that prove?' he shouted. 'Individuals who were even more faithful and devoted than he have committed worse crimes! The past doesn't count. Every day you see devoted fathers leaving their wives and children for some piece of fluff... And cashiers, after years of faithful service, absconding with the cash. Who's to say, mon cher substitut, that one of us won't commit a crime tomorrow? Don't protest!... You don't know anything, and neither do I. It all depends on the circumstances.'

There was a knock on the door.

'Monsieur le juge d'instruction,' said the newcomer. 'The cripple has asked to speak to you personally.'

'Show him in!... Even the slightest testimonies are interesting. We might learn something from what the retard tells us. After all, the cackling of geese saved Rome.'

Proud of his classical allusion, M. Launay gave a satisfied laugh.

Clodoche came in, trailing his crutch behind him.

The magistrate looked at him with curiosity, then asked him gently:

'What do you want, my friend?'

The cripple responded:

'Clodoche wishes to speak to monsieur le juge, because Clodoche found something in the fountain.'

He delved into the vast pocket of his blue gardening apron and pulled out a revolver, which he placed on the table.

M. Launay picked up the weapon and examined it.

'A regulation revolver, calibre eight millimetres. There's no doubt this is the murder weapon,' he murmured.

The superintendent grumbled:

'What a pity this exhibit was picked up by that imbecile. He will have blurred the fingerprints.'

M. Launay erupted:

'It's the fault of your inspectors, Pruvost! They should have found it a long time ago... Clodoche picked it up quite naturally, without precautions... and it's going to be difficult for us to find any traces of the murderer.'

The superintendent muttered:

'I only have two inspectors under my command. One was watching the butler in the small salon and the other hasn't had time to visit the entire property.'

'It's always the same thing,' shouted the magistrate. 'You don't see anything. You wear yourself out on pointless details and you overlook the truth which is staring you in the face! A simple peasant discovers an item of vital importance... And where? In the fountain, in the park, right in the middle of the central driveway. A place you must have gone past twenty times. If you'd found it at the start of the investigation, you could have brought it to me delicately. Then I would now have the criminal's fingerprints, a crucial proof.'

'But, monsieur le juge d'instruction....'

'There are no buts. You hinder the course of the justice that it's your job to serve. If, because of your clumsiness, the fingerprints are blurred, I shall report you to the minister. And you'll be dismissed!'

M. Launay emphasised his point by bringing his fist down hard on the table.

Suspecting vaguely that he was the indirect cause of the anger, the unhappy Clodoche rolled his eyes and regarded M. Launay anxiously.

The magistrate's outbursts were violent, but of short duration. He calmed down quickly and addressed the superintendent, who had weathered the storm with his head down:

'Pruvost, stop your investigation immediately and place your second inspector at the door of this residence, with orders only to let out persons carrying written permission from me. Now, go!'

The superintendent exited, taking Clodoche, stunned by his unexpected reception, with him.

The deputy had been stroking his beard in silence, his gaze obscured by his pince-nez.

He broke his silence to address M. Launay:

'Another complication! Nothing is going smoothly. It's a dead end we'll never get out of!'

'I don't share your pessimism,' retorted the magistrate. 'Obviously, there are still a few small points to clear up, but overall it's not going badly, not badly at all. And I congratulate myself for arriving in time to correct Lieutenant Taupinois's blunders. What say you, Monsieur Dupont-Lesguyères?'

Recalling the bad moments he had experienced at the hands of the gendarme officer, the secretary smiled amiably at the perceptive magistrate, even though he couldn't quite see to what extent the investigation had advanced since the arrival of M. Launay.

Only too happy to be free of suspicion, Adhémar demanded nothing more for the moment.

He listened complacently to the explanations which the magistrate was giving to the deputy.

'I've never abandoned certain basic principles,' continued M. Launay pompously. And I can't complain, because once again those principles are leading me to the truth today.'

He lit a cigar and continued:

'The first basic principle I adopted is to find out who profited from the crime. *Is fecit cui prodest*, to quote Seneca.'

M. Malicorne nodded approvingly.

The magistrate continued:

'Let us look at the victim's entourage. Whom do we see?... Old servants, all devoted to their master. A superficial mind would have stopped there and looked elsewhere. That's not the case with me! I asked myself why, for that very reason, the investigation shouldn't be limited to the domestic circle.'

M. Launay turned to the secretary.

'Of course, Monsieur Dupont-Lesguyères, I exclude you, and the suspicions of a mere gendarme will not influence my opinion.'

Adhémar bowed and the magistrate continued:

'My task became easier after I learnt, thanks to your hints, Monsieur Dupont-Lesguyères, that Charles Chapon, the butler, was the principal heir to the deceased's estate. All that was left was to examine the facts. Which is what I did.'

'In this instance, the facts are far from obvious,' observed the deputy acidly.

'That's not my opinion, Monsieur Malicorne! There's one fact that emerges from all the diverse questioning that you've observed. All the witnesses are in agreement with each other. At the present time I can describe the crime as if I had been there myself.'

The magistrate took his listeners into the entrance hall.

'We're here,' he said, 'at the scene of the crime. Imagine we've gone back in time to the evening of October 28. Gustave Colinet and Edmond and Jeanne Tasseau are in their rooms on the top floor. Verdinage is upstairs, and Charles is on the ground floor. Thérèse is on her usual rounds, checking that no villain is hiding in the house, and that the doors and windows are hermetically sealed. She goes to bed as well, and after a brief period of watch, hands over the duty to her husband and falls asleep.'

'We're in agreement so far,' said M. Malicorne.

'So far, the night of October 28 is uneventful, just like any other night. Then the drama begins. Phase one: at about midnight Verdinage surreptitiously leaves his rooms and installs himself noiselessly in the library. Such precautions become understandable, once you know how careful the lord of the manor had been to hide the news of the letter containing the death warrant from his staff. *At a quarter past twelve, Verdinage was still awaiting* the arrival of his mysterious correspondent, as we know from the note he scribbled at the bottom of the letter, the famous third letter, as you can see for yourselves.'

M. Launay showed the deputy and the secretary the typed page, at the bottom of which had been written in pencil:

"Quarter past midnight... nothing."

'It's definitely my master's handwriting,' confirmed Adhémar.

The magistrate continued:

'Phase two. Let us leave Verdinage in the library and go to the adjoining room, that of the Chapons. The butler, leaving his sleeping wife, goes down to the cellar. At least, that's what Charles claims. It's impossible, for now, to verify his testimony. Which is "really bad luck," as the saying goes. The only assertion that it would be useful to corroborate is precisely *the only one* without another witness. Let us not dwell on that point and let us simply register that, at the time that the crime is about to happen, Charles Chapon is somewhere in the hall.'

The deputy, stroking his fine beard, objected:

'But, monsieur le juge, Charles claims he was down in the cellar.'

M. Launay smiled sweetly and replied offhandedly:

'You seem to forget, Monsieur Malicorne, that Verdinage was waiting in the library and had turned the electricity on. The lord of the manor had undoubtedly left the door to the hallway open in order to better hear the arrival of his visitor.'

'That is indeed plausible.'

There was a rush of blood to the magistrate's face.

'What do you mean, plausible?' he shouted. 'What you mean is that it's logical, certain, incontestable!'

'All right,' replied the deputy soothingly. He abhorred argument and had, incidentally, a completely different opinion as to the identity of the criminal.

'Once you accept my theory,' continued M. Launay, 'how can you imagine that Charles, who hid in order to drink, would have been reckless enough to have gone down to the cellar when his master—whom he knew to be awake and a few steps away—could have caught him in flagrant drunkenness?'

'Charles could have gone down to the cellar before M. Verdinage went into the library,' observed Adhémar.

'In any case, the butler was on the alert, ready to come out of the cellar the moment he heard his master return upstairs.'

'Obviously, monsieur le juge.'

'Third phase,' announced M. Launay.

He stood in front of them, his hands in his pockets, and continued:

'We are now at the heart of the drama. Clodoche brings the stranger to the front door, puts his lantern down on the step and waits. Verdinage opens the door to let in his nocturnal visitor and closes it behind him. The first words out of the lord of the manor's mouth are to affirm vehemently to the writer of the anonymous letters: "No! I won't leave!"'

'Those were indeed the words Thérèse heard,' murmured the deputy.

Adhémar asked hesitantly:

'Could the murderer be someone familiar with the mansion, a...?'

'Let's keep going,' interrupted the magistrate. 'The killer fires on his host, who has preceded him into the library. The owner, fatally wounded, falls to the floor and expires. The crime has been accomplished.'

The deputy and the secretary were listening attentively.

The magistrate pointed to the door connecting the library and the hallway.

'The murderer is there,' he said. 'There's only one way he can leave: through the same front door by which he entered the manor. But that way out is blocked because, on the other side of the door, Clodoche is on guard, banging with his crutch and shouting.'

'And then?' asked Adhémar.

'The killer couldn't escape through the front because Clodoche was blocking the way and Gustave, leaning out of his window, was watching the park.

'He couldn't have hidden in one of the ground floor rooms, *which were all visited twice*—the first time by the chauffeur Tasseau, accompanied by Clodoche, and the second time by the gendarmes. And finally, he couldn't reach the upstairs floors, because he would have met three people in succession on the staircase: Edmond Tasseau, Gustave Colinet, and Jeanne Tasseau.'

'That leaves the cellar,' suggested the deputy, proud of his perspicacity.

'You've hit the nail on the head, Monsieur Malicorne! *That leaves the cellar.* That's the only possibility. If, as he claims, Charles Chapon was down there, he must have seen the murderer come down and let him hide there.'

'That's undeniable!' echoed the deputy.

'Furthermore,' continued M. Launay, 'whereas Edmond Tasseau and Clodoche both visited the ground floor, the butler—*and only the butler—visited the cellar and locked the door with the key that only he possessed, as if he feared that one of the other servants might try to come down.*'

'So you're admitting the complicity of Charles Chapon?' asked the frightened secretary.

'I don't see any other way of explaining what happened,' concluded the magistrate.

'But,' observed M. Malicorne, 'with the murderer shut in the cellar, the door was only re-opened in the presence of the gendarmes. And the subsequent orderly search was performed by Lieutenant Taupinois himself.'

'That,' retorted M. Launay sententiously, 'is the only point which remains to be clarified. *How and when did Charles Chapon allow the murderer to escape?*'

VI

The magistrate, his head back, his eyes on the ceiling, and his thumbs tucked into his waistcoat, held forth confidently:

'As I see it, it's less about knowing *who* committed the crime than determining *how* it was done. It's undeniable that Clodoche led someone from the park gate to Marchenoire Manor. That's now a duly-established fact that does not need revisiting. If there were any remaining doubt, we only have to look at the testimony of all those present in the house on the evening of October 28. *They all saw or heard the arrival of the murderer and his guide.*'

M. Launay, happy to be able to express his point of view without fear of contradiction, continued his argument:

'Clodoche, having led the visitor Verdinage was expecting, mounted guard in front of the door, in strict accordance with the instructions he had been given. The witness Colinet, Gustave, saw him alone on the steps, *therefore the mysterious person did indeed enter the manor.* That's a second duly established fact. Now follow my reasoning....'

The magistrate looked condescendingly at his audience, leaving no doubt as to the certitude of his reasoning, but the superintendent, refusing to budge, interrupted him:

'We know the murderer, led by Clodoche, entered the mansion and could not be found on the premises after the crime, so we must accept that he left. And there was only one way he could have done that: *by going out the same way he came in!* And who guarded the exit? ... Clodoche.'

The magistrate, extremely agitated, shouted:

'What, Pruvost? Are you suggesting that the miserable retard was an accomplice?'

The superintendent, unfazed by the outburst, replied calmly:

'Why not?'

With a note of defiance in his voice, he repeated:

'Yes, why not?... Oh, I'm not suggesting that the *minus habens* was capable of planning such a murder, but it's not impossible that, under pressure, he became the killer's accomplice.

'Let's not forget Verdinage's pencilled note: *"Quarter past midnight... nothing."* Isn't it reasonable to suppose that *if the visitor was making him wait, it was because he was negotiating with Clodoche?'*

'But he told the gendarmes that he led the visitor from the park gate without a single word being exchanged, and only uttered the words Verdinage had taught him to say, once they arrived at the manor.'

The magistrate's words, delivered with an ironic smile, prompted M. Pruvost to respond:

'He told the gendarmes and they believed him. I have a feeling that, when Clodoche is interviewed by a more perceptive interrogator, it won't be so easy to mislead him. There's a slight difference between a superintendent worthy of the name and a lieutenant in the gendarmerie which is not to the police's advantage.'

M. Launay remained coldly silent, but M. Malicorne nodded his agreement.

M. Pruvost concluded emphatically:

'There's no longer a mystery if we look at the obvious truth: the murderer who entered Marchenoire Manor did not mysteriously disappear, but left in the most natural way possible, thanks to the obvious complicity of our friend Clodoche!'

With infinite condescension, the magistrate appeared to consider the superintendent's arguments and replied:

'We shall see. My dear Pruvost... We shall see.'

He turned to the gendarme on duty and ordered him to bring the cripple in immediately.

On seeing the unfortunate fellow, whose face reflected an almost total imbecility, dragging himself forward, the magistrate had a momentary pang of pity. Clodoche simply did not look like someone who could plot, or even be an accomplice to, a crime. The stupid oaf must have executed his master's orders to the letter. If in fact he had been guilty in some way, he was too simple-minded not to be confused in his replies.

M. Launay waited confidently for the interrogation Pruvost was preparing, happy at the thought that the superintendent was sadly mistaken.

André Prevost peppered the cripple relentlessly with questions:

'When he arrived at the park gate where you were waiting, on the evening of October 28 at around midnight, the person whom you were responsible for taking to your master spoke a few words to you, did they not?'

'Words?'

'Yes, that person spoke to you, did they not?'

'No, monsieur commissaire.'

'They did at least say "Bonsoir," did they not?'

'No, monsieur commissaire, not "Bonsoir."'

'But you yourself, Clodoche, you must have greeted the visitor.'

'Yes, monsieur commissaire: like this!'

Clodoche reached for his vast straw hat and removed it clumsily, as was his custom when addressed.

'And the stranger replied "Bonsoir,"' insisted M. Pruvost.

'No, monsieur commissaire.'

'Very well. On the way up, did the person you were leading talk about... the heavy rain?'

'No, monsieur commissaire.'

'But you yourself did try to start a conversation?'

'The good master told Clodoche to lead the "someone," but didn't ask Clodoche to talk to the "someone."'

'Of course. But M. Verdinage didn't forbid you to reply. What did you say to the visitor after he spoke to you?'

'The "someone" didn't speak to Clodoche.'

'You say that he didn't speak to you, but on his arrival at the gate you said....'

'"Follow me to the manor. You're expected." That's what the good master told Clodoche to say to the "someone."'

'And the "someone," as you call him, replied: "Yes."'

'The "someone" didn't reply. He just followed Clodoche.'

M. Pruvost stopped, visibly disappointed. The cripple's sincerity was obvious. There was no contradiction in his replies, no matter how many different ways the questions were put.

The superintendent did not accept he was beaten, and pushed on relentlessly:

'Are you sure the door was shut behind the visitor as soon as he had entered?'

''Yes, monsieur commissaire. Clodoche saw the good master, who

103

opened the door to the "someone," close it himself and make a sign to Clodoche... like that.'

The cripple made a gesture with his hand, supposedly the one Verdinage had made, to indicate he should wait outside until further notice.

The superintendent continued, not letting up:

'After the shot, the manor door opened suddenly; the person you had led to see M. Verdinage came out in a hurry, pushed you aside, and left.'

'No, monsieur commissaire, no!'

'Then they came out just at the moment when someone, from the inside, opened the door to you.'

'Oh! no, monsieur commissaire!... Clodoche would have seen and would have stopped the "someone" from leaving... That's what the good master told Clodoche to do.'

'Anyone can be afraid, Clodoche. You were afraid of the killer who had just fired a revolver shot and, fearful of sharing your master's fate, you allowed him to escape. He may even have threatened you with his weapon.'

'No! No! No! Monsieur commissaire... Clodoche would have hit the "someone!"'

Supporting himself with one hand on the desk, the cripple brandished his crutch menacingly with the other.

The investigators—whilst thinking that the cripple could easily have been pushed over—all felt certain that he would at least have tried to defend his master, for whom he seemed to have the affection of a large guard dog.

Despite appearances, M. André Pruvost was not the kind of man to abandon an idea before becoming convinced that he was wrong. Having floated the idea of Clodoche being an accomplice—willing or not—he was extremely reluctant to abandon it. The sarcastic smile of the magistrate broadened with each of Clodoche's responses.

With a gesture of annoyance, the superintendent dismissed the cripple and, after Clodoche had left, turned to M. Launay, who was whistling complacently:

'With your permission, monsieur le juge,' he said furiously, 'I shall question Clodoche again. I shall question him ten times. Twenty, if I must!... and we shall see whether he confesses, if not to his guilt, at

104

least to a moment of cowardice.'

'What the devil?' retorted the other. 'You still intend to demonstrate the complicity of that dolt?'

'What do you mean, do I still intend?' replied the superintendent in astonishment. 'When Clodoche admits he let the murderer escape there'll be no more mystery, because we shall know how the individual who entered the *forbidden house* escaped from it.'

With a pitying smile, M. Launay replied:

'Others may have an opinion about the crime which, whilst differing from yours, is no less plausible. Is it really necessary, in order to explain what seems to be a mystery, to accept that the murderer left by whence he came?'

'But....'

'Not at all!... My dear Provost, you forget that the criminal could have hidden himself somewhere, and probably did not attempt to leave immediately after his crime.'

'But the house was searched from top to bottom!'

The magistrate blew a puff of smoke at the ceiling whilst emitting a slight whistle of incredulity.

'My dear fellow,' he replied, after a moment's reflection, 'there's the cellar... *The cellar, which only Charles Chapon explored.* Think whatever you like—that's your right—but don't try to prevent others from thinking that the killer's accomplice was not Clodoche: it was Charles Chapon!'

M. Launay had spoken pompously and turned to the deputy for approval.

M. Malicorne nodded his head as usual, but without conviction because he, too, had an opinion about the tragedy at Marchenoire, and for him the culprit was neither Clodoche nor Charles Chapon: it was Jacques Bénard!

VII

That Sunday afternoon, Octave Balutin was partaking of small sips of the mediocre coffee that his sister Adélaïde had frugally prepared.

The latter, an old maid with angular, dry features bustled about the dining room with small steps, sweeping up crumbs and collecting dishes, glasses and bottles silently, so as not to interrupt the tinny sounds from the loudspeaker, which was broadcasting the most popular air from the opera *Louise*.

Everything in the room was second-rate: the furniture, the framed prints, the radio with the sound quality of a bad gramophone.

The sound of the doorbell caused the Balutins to look at each other in astonishment. Who could be visiting them on a Sunday afternoon? They had no friends: Octave's meagre salary as an accountant in a third-rate export company didn't allow them to throw parties. Nevertheless, their eyes lit up when the same thought occurred to both of them:

'Suppose it's about the inheritance?'

Adélaïde, having cautiously opened the front door, found herself face to face with a small, clean-shaven, slightly pot-bellied man wearing a monocle, whose long, curly hair was pulled back to the nape of his neck.

Twirling his hat in his fingers, the visitor bowed deeply and murmured, in a smooth, musical voice:

'Tom Morrow, Director of the A.P.P., Agence de Police Privée, at your service.'

Trembling with emotion, and with a lump in her throat, the old maid replied:

'Come in, monsieur.'

The little man bowed once again smilingly and waited for Mlle. Balutin to invite him into the dining room, which also served as a salon.

Noticing Octave, the policeman introduced himself for the second time and sat down on the chair he was offered.

His fleshy lips retained their pleasant smile as he removed his

107

gloves to reveal pale white hands with carefully polished nails.

'Mademoiselle, monsieur,' he began, 'you may have already guessed why I have taken the liberty of disturbing your domestic peace?'

So saying, he pointed with a chubby finger at the radio, where a voice was reading an advertisement for furniture.

Octave shut off the appliance and stammered:

'No... I mean yes, monsieur....'

'Tom Morrow,' the detective replied obligingly.

Full of good humour, he added:

'I'm pleased to see that we understand each other perfectly. I've come to inform you about an inheritance which is of great interest to you: that of Napoléon Verdinage, mysteriously murdered in his manor in Marchenoire.'

'Our poor cousin,' sighed the old maid, feigning heartfelt sadness.

'Such a good relative!' echoed Octave.

Tom Morrow, looking quickly around, took note of the modest décor, but refrained from observing that the "such a good relative" appeared to have thought very little about helping his financially impoverished cousins. He bowed solemnly in the face of the insincere grief of the Balutins, as if to offer them discreet condolences, and continued:

'I'm sure you're aware, mademoiselle and monsieur , that the late Napoléon Verdinage, before being attacked in the manner all the newspapers are talking about, had left numerous wills. The latest, and the only valid one, is in the hands of Me. Laridoire, a lawyer in Compiègne.'

The old maid could no longer contain her resentment.

'To treat us like that! Us... his only relatives,' she shouted angrily.

'I thought you were distant cousins?' asked the policeman timidly.

Octave took it upon himself to reply, bitterly:

'Distant cousins, but cousins all the same! Verdinage, as my sister just explained, has no other relatives apart from ourselves... If he'd had any family values—values which every feeling man should possess—he would not have committed that....'

'That act of infamy!' interjected Adélaïde, slapping the table with her dry yellow hand.

Tom Morrow, still calm, replied gently:

'I see that you've been reading about all the details of the investigation led by M.Launay, juge d'instruction, assisted by M. André Pruvost, commissionnaire divisionnaire, M. Paul Malicorne, substitut du Procureur de la République and Lieutenant Taupinois of the gendarmerie régionale. You know, therefore, that your cousin left the bulk of his estate to be divided amongst his servants.'

Once again, the old maid erupted angrily and remarked with a sneer:

'As if those servants hadn't fleeced him enough whilst he was alive!... That will is the height of absurdity and ignominy... It deprives good people like his relatives for the benefit of those unspeakable flunkeys.'

Octave Balutin piled it on: 'For thirty years, my sister and I have lived frugally on my earnings... Fate, which smiles on some, never bestowed us any favours. Just as Providence was about to reward our years of toil, an immoral will—and immoral is the right word, monsieur—deprives us of our well-earned affluence.'

Tom Morrow asked artfully:

'And were your relations with your distant cousin... distant?'

Adélaïde retorted sharply:

'Obviously! We were no longer "of the same world"... We had lost sight of each other over the years, but when our cousin founded the grocers' association of Montrouge we tried to renew our family ties. Verdinage responded favourably, I must admit, but he never thought to let us profit from the excessive luxury in which he wallowed.'

'He was an arriviste,' sneered Octave contemptuously.

'Be that as it may,' replied the smiling policeman, running a hand through his hair, 'one thing is clear: the servants of the late Verdinage are going to be sharing a pretty penny.'

Mlle. Balutin smiled hatefully, revealing her long, yellow teeth. It seemed that Tom Morrow felt that the time was ripe, for he suddenly decided to reveal the object of his visit.

'In my opinion,' he declared, 'it's not impossible to ensure that the late Napoléon Verdinage's inheritance does not go to his servants, and, as a consequence all, or almost all, of it would go to you.'

The Balutins reacted as if they had received an electric shock. Their eyes gleamed with avarice as they regarded the little man who had just given them such wild hope.

109

'What did you say?' gasped the brother, turning pale.

'I said,' replied the detective, stroking his hair nonchalantly, 'that it's possible that the victim's servants might not legally be able to lay claim to your cousin's estate, in which case you would be the sole beneficiaries.'

'But how?' exclaimed the old maid, who could hardly contain her agonised impatience.

'Quite simply,' retorted the other. 'It's obvious that if we could show, for example, that Verdinage was murdered by his servants, or because of their complicity, there would be no question of allowing them to benefit from their crime.'

'Obviously!' exclaimed the accountant triumphantly.

Adélaïde rushed to the policeman's side and clutched his hands effusively.

'Thank you, monsieur, for telling us that and for giving us hope,' she said. 'We told each other, Octave and I, that Heaven would not permit good people to be robbed.'

'What's more,' added Balutin, 'the investigators have proved the guilt of those wretches. We're saved!'

To the great astonishment of Verdinage's cousins, Tom Morrow declared:

'The investigators have proved nothing whatsoever!'

Octave recoiled:

'What?... The juge d'instruction demonstrated Charles Chapon's guilt as an accomplice; the substitut du Procureur de la République accused Jacques Bénard; and the commissionnaire divisionnaire insisted it was Clodoche.'

With a benevolent smile, the director of the Agence de Police Privée insisted:

'It's for that very reason that I say they haven't proved anything at all!'

Anticipating indignant protests from his audience, Tom Morrow added:

'Let us examine the contradictory conclusion of these three gentlemen, after which I intend to demonstrate that *even the best of their hypotheses explains absolutely nothing.'*

The little man smoothed his hair in silence for a few moments and began:

110

'M. Launay's belief in the guilt of the butler Charles Chapon is based on the contradictions and reticence in his own testimony, as much as those of his wife, Thérèse. But all of that, legally speaking, is perfectly meaningless unless M. Launay can explain *how* the butler helped the murderer to escape after the crime.'

The faces of the Balutins, who had never thought of the "how," registered astonishment. The policeman continued:

'M. Paul Malicorne believes in the guilt of the guard, Jacques Bénard. Here again, nothing has been proved. One can only reproach the guard for his persistent urging that Verdinage leave Marchenoire Manor. But M. Malicorne has not shown, any more than M. Launay, *how* the murderer left the scene of the crime.'

Without apparently having noticed the consternation of his audience, Tom Morrow continued:

'Lieutenant Taupinois set his heart on M. le Marquis Adhémar Dupont-Lesguyères, secretary of the deceased. He couldn't show *how* the murderer left the scene of the crime either.'

The policeman concluded:

'As long as we cannot prove conclusively the "how," we haven't proved anything!'

Octave Balutin, who could hardly contain himself, picked up a newspaper and thrust it under the detective's nose.

'You forget, monsieur, the most damning hypothesis, that of M. André Pruvost.'

Tom Morrow folded the newspaper without even looking at it and replied with a smile:

'*His hypothesis is no more valid than any of the others* if you stop and examine it seriously. M. Pruvost accuses Clodoche. Let's think about that....'

The little man leant towards his listeners, who were waiting agog on his every pronouncement:

'The first hypothesis is that Clodoche, either out of self-interest or stupidity—you see that I'm exploring all possibilities!—allowed the murderer, whom he had previously escorted to his master, to escape. But Gustave Colinet, who was watching from his window, was a witness and would have seen the killer's escape.'

Adélaïde interrupted him vehemently.

'He didn't just say Clodoche was a witness. He formally accused

111

him of being the murderer.'

'Very well,' conceded Tom Morrow, bowing yet again. 'Let's suppose that Clodoche killed Verdinage, even though it would be quite surprising that an idiot, who is also a cripple, could have planned such a crime.'

The old maid was adamant:

'M. Pruvost, however....'

'Let's suppose,' conceded the policeman amicably. 'Let's suppose that it was Clodoche who, from the front steps, fired on Verdinage and killed him. Apart from the findings of the medical examiner—who showed that the bullet was not fired from so far away—let us not forget that Clodoche led the mysterious visitor, for whom he had waited at the gate, up to the manor where the late Verdinage himself opened the door. A door whose lock did not open from the outside.'

'Agreed. So what?' asked the accountant.

'So what?' repeated the detective placidly, 'I would like M. Pruvost to explain how the mysterious visitor could have left *the forbidden house. If he had armed Clodoche, why did he need to enter the manor, from which it would be impossible to leave?* Let us not forget that *no one saw him leave, even though multiple witnesses saw him enter.* Whether we like it or not, the problem can be summarized in a few words:

'"A man went in... how did he get out?"'

'So,' stammered Adélaïde Balutin, 'according to you, Clodoche...'

'*... Is neither the murderer nor the accomplice,*' said the policeman, finishing the sentence.

Octave, disconcerted by the detective's irrefutable logic, murmured:

'If none of those hypotheses is correct, is there no other solution?'

Smiling even more broadly, Tom Morrow declared:

'On the contrary, I believe there is a solution, *the only one possible.*'

'The complicity of all the servants together,' suggested Octave.

'No,' replied the little man. 'No... *something else.*'

Pleading now, the old maid implored him, her hands locked together:

'And... what is that something else?'

Tom Morrow bowed gallantly before responding:

112

'It's something that I will be happy to explain, if... if we can come to agreement on certain purely material questions.'

Looking askance at him, Adélaïde hissed:

'Blackmail?'

Without batting an eyelid, the policeman answered gently:

'Never, mademoiselle, never... Merely a just remuneration for my efforts.'

Octave stood up:

'Monsieur, when the case comes before the court, the jury, after listening to the theories of the various investigators, will believe one or several of the servants guilty...'

'Unless I tell the jury that the theories are false and don't explain anything, just as I've just demonstrated to you. Then no one will be found guilty and the inheritance....'

'You won't do that!' screamed the old maid furiously. 'You must let the juries find them guilty!'

'Out of the question, mademoiselle,' replied Tom Morrow, his hand on his heart and his eyes raised to the ceiling. 'My conscience would never allow an innocent man to be found guilty!'

There was a long silence, during which the cousins, pale and tense, looked at each other questioningly. Then Octave sat down, hesitated, coughed nervously, and asked:

'Very well, monsieur, it's agreed. We accept your services. How much?'

Tom Morrow, Director of the A.P.P, had won.

VIII

The medical examiner having issued the burial permit, Verdinage's funeral could now take place.

The body lay in state as the Balutin cousins, wizened and bony, appearing shrunken in their black clothes, Me. Laridoire, whose professional solemnity made a considerable impression, and the directors of the grocers' association of Montrouge paid tribute to Verdinage's mortal remains.

Then the park gate was thrown open and the inhabitants of the village were allowed to file past to pay their respects. Separate groups formed, comprising the ladies of the communal wash house and the drinkers at the *Ménard jeune*.

Everyone marvelled at the lavish surroundings, ordered by the grocer himself in the first paragraph of his will.

There was talk also of the *forbidden house*; the majority of the villagers cursed the butler and the cripple, accused of complicity in the murder.

Only two voices were raised in favour of Charles and Clodoche: those of La Perette and le père Lafinette.

According to them, the magistrate had been wrong to treat the mysterious happenings of October 28 as a criminal matter.

'The devil was involved!' claimed La Perette, crossing herself.

Le père Lafinette, a free thinker, stopped short of blaming Hell. He declared, rather more vaguely:

'No man could have done that!'

Grouped around the coffin of their master, the servants were crying. Thérèse, slumped in a chair, sobbed uncontrollably, oblivious to everything but her own suffering.

Adhémar Dupont-Lesguyères assumed the role of lord of the manor, giving orders to Gustave, Edmond and Jeanne, shaking the hands of the directors, patting the lawyer on the shoulder, and kissing the fingers of old cousin Adélaïde.

After that, the hearse left for the cemetery of Père-Lachaise in Paris, where the grocer had built a sumptuous vault for himself. A

115

limousine crammed with the cousins, the directors, the lawyer, Adhémar, and Thérèse followed behind.

It looked as though the housemaid-nanny was about to succumb to the double tragedy which had struck her, as her mind wandered between the loss of her beloved "Napo," so cruelly assassinated, and the fate of her husband, arrested and under lock and key as the result of an odious allegation.

According to her, Clodoche was solely responsible for the murder, for she could never believe that Charles was guilty. It was true that, under the influence, he occasionally lost his mind, but that weakness would never have caused him to commit a murder—and what a murder! That of his benefactor.

Nevertheless, the peculiar attitude of her spouse on the night of the crime disconcerted Thérèse.

What troubled her most was the question:

Why did Charles go down to the cellar that night? Agreed, the temptation to open a few bottles was irresistible, *but was that really the only reason?*

She dared not answer that agonising question and would rather have died on the spot than think about such a nightmare.

....

M. Launay, too, wished to be rid of the whole business.

But, despite subjecting Charles to two more interrogations, the butler remained mute, repeating endlessly:

'It wasn't me! It wasn't me!'

As for Clodoche, he continued to give unintelligible responses to the questions posed by the superintendent, who continued to believe in his guilt.

The two accused had each been provided with a defence lawyer: Me. Lebrument, a portly gentleman with a patriarch's beard, a blank expression, and an imperturbable manner, whose constant movement of the lower jaw made him appear to be a species of ruminant; and Me. Chaumel, a recent graduate, fresh from law school and full of passion, whose insurmountable timidity made him terrified of the magistrate's sudden outbursts.

The latter had not given up hope of making Charles Chapon confess and thus learning, not only *how* the murderer escaped, but *who* was the mysterious visitor that the butler had helped.

The magistrate could already envision the flattering newspaper articles about the rapid and decisive success. His picture would be on the front page, accompanied by articles glorifying his perspicacity in bringing such a complex case to a just conclusion. He would be "M. Claude Launay, the young and energetic magistrate from Compiègne, who is credited with solving the mystery of *the forbidden house*."

And, after a brief delay, there would be celebrity, glory and rapid promotion!

Puffing out his chest, the magistrate smiled heavenwards.

He paced up and down his chambers whilst his clerk Ernest compiled a thick dossier and the deputy dreamily stroked his beard.

Suddenly the door opened and the superintendent appeared.

The policeman placed the regulation revolver that Clodoche had found in the fountain on the table.

'I've just come from Marchenoire,' he announced. 'I showed this weapon to several of the servants. They all confirm that *the revolver belongs to Jacques Bénard.*'

'To the guard Jacques Bénard!' repeated M. Malicorne.

The deputy asked dispassionately:

'Is this revolver, belonging to Jacques   Bénard, the murder weapon?'

'The weapons expert Durand is convinced it is. The scratches on the bullet which killed Verdinage can be traced back to the barrel of this revolver.'

The magistrate turned to his clerk:

'Has the criminal records office completed its report?'

'It came in this morning,' replied Ernest. 'There are photographs of two separate sets of fingerprints.'

After consulting the report M. Launay announced:

'*The first set of prints belong to Clodoche.*'

'He's the murderer! The prints are the proof!' exclaimed Pruvost, whose theory seemed to be justified.

'I don't think so,' retorted M. Launay. 'You seem to forget it was he who retrieved the revolver from the fountain and handed it over without taking any precautions. So it's perfectly natural that his fingerprints are on it.'

The superintendent was at a loss for words.

'And whose are the second prints?' asked M. Malicorne casually.

'*They belong to Bénard,*' replied the magistrate.

'I thought as much,' murmured the deputy.

Lighting a cigar, M. Launay asked Pruvost:

'So, when you showed the murder weapon to Verdinage's servants, did all of them recognise it as belonging to Bénard?'

'Bénard himself recognised it. He could hardly do otherwise!'

'I imagine that, as a consequence, you've gathered more information about the guard?'

'Of course. I questioned M. Dupont-Lesguyères upon his return from Paris, where he had attended the burial of his master. M. Dupont-Lesguyères doesn't know Bénard very well and simply repeated his earlier testimony, namely that Bénard has only been in Verdinage's employ since he bought Marchenoire. M. Dupont-Lesguyères told me that Verdinage hardly spoke to Bénard, whom he didn't like very much.'

'Well, that's interesting!' observed M. Malicorne. 'And what is the basis for the secretary's statement?'

'On certain confidential remarks Verdinage made. Apparently he made clear, several times, his intention to dismiss Bénard.'

'What didn't he like about the man?'

'Nothing in particular, but he commented that Bénard was incorrigibly lazy and that he'd hired the poor cripple Clodoche, less out of charity than to give him most of the work. The way Clodoche was treated appalled Verdinage, who was only waiting for the right moment to give Bénard the sack.'

'Were those the only reasons for his antipathy towards Bénard?'

'M. Dupont-Lesguyères believes that his master felt the guard attached too much importance to the threatening letters. There was even a violent argument on the subject which was overheard by all the servants.'

The deputy wrote down a few observations, then asked the superintendent:

'And what was the subject of the violent argument?'

'Bénard was begging the lord of the manor to obey the letter-writer's orders and leave *the forbidden house.*'

'*So Bénard was insisting that Verdinage leave?*'

'He insisted several times, in fact, and each time Verdinage became angrier. It may have been out of simple bravado that the lord of the manor refused to leave.'

'Perfect! Perfect!' chortled M. Malicorne. 'There's a disturbing pattern of suspicious activity.'

'Disturbing?' muttered the magistrate.

'Particularly,' continued the deputy, 'since, amongst all Verdinage's servants: M. Dupont-Lesguyères, Charles and Thérèse Chapon, Edmond and Jeanne Tasseau, Gustave Colinet and Clodoche, Jacques Bénard was the *only* one living in the manor when M. Desrousseaux was murdered for not obeying orders to leave, *just like Verdinage!*'

'Just like Verdinage,' repeated Pruvost.

'If you put it like that...' conceded M. Launay.

The deputy pressed harder.

'Bénard is guilty! He's the only one who could have murdered Desrousseaux! He alone murdered Verdinage, for the same reason. He murdered Desrousseaux with a rifle shot but Verdinage, surrounded by his servants, was more difficult to kill. The guard found an accomplice in Charles Chapon, ready to do anything to protect the inheritance he risked losing.'

'Charles Chapon is complicit! There's no doubt about it!' crowed the magistrate, all too ready to accept any theory that confirmed his own point of view.

The superintendent refused to accept that he was beaten:

'Why couldn't Bénard be Clodoche's accomplice?' he asked.

'Because Clodoche had nothing to gain from his master's death!' retorted M. Malicorne.

'Clodoche is under lock and key, and I intend to study his case closely!' interjected M. Launay.

The magistrate signed an appearance summons with the guard's name on it and handed it to Pruvost.

An inspector came in with a visiting card.

'Tom Morrow, Director of the A.P.P.'' said M. Launay. 'What does this amateur policeman want?'

Tom Morrow entered on tiptoe, ran a hand through his hair and bowed:

'Monsieur le juge, I believe?'

'Correct,' replied M. Launay coldly.

'May I speak in front of these messieurs?' asked the other, indicating M. Malicorne and Ernest.

'Yes, but make it quick. What do you want?'

The private detective bowed again:

'I've learnt,' he said in a musical voice, 'I've learnt, monsieur le juge, how skilfully you've cleared up the mystery of *the forbidden house.*'

'The main points, at least,' replied M. Launay modestly.

'Monsieur le juge,' continued Tom Morrow unctuously, 'I'm proud to acknowledge you as one of only a dozen magistrates who honour the system of justice of our beloved country. I say that as one who knows the difficulties of the profession which you exercise so brilliantly.'

M. Launay wanted to respond to the compliments with mild protests—even though he was aware that he fully deserved them—but the private detective did not give him the opportunity:

'No protests, please!' he exclaimed. 'There are times when modesty itself is a crime. It's important that you know your own worth.'

'My goodness, monsieur,' replied the magistrate, bowing in turn. 'I try my best. I see things clearly and I flatter myself there's method to my work. That's all. To what do I owe the honour of your visit?'

'It's very simple, monsieur le juge. The heirs to M. Verdinage's estate intend to file a civil action. They have asked me to follow the case as a simple observer.'

'But the principal heir is Charles Chapon, who has been charged as an accomplice to the murder.'

'Precisely! That's why the legal heirs of the deceased want to nullify the will.'

'Obviously, a criminal cannot benefit from his crime,' conceded M. Launay. 'As far as my investigation is concerned, I would be happy to keep you abreast of any results and have you attend the hearing, which will take place tomorrow.'

'I would expect no less of a man of your courtesy.'

'Here's where things stand,' said the magistrate, lighting a cigar and blowing a puff of smoke at the ceiling.

'Personally,' he continued, 'I believe that Charles Chapon is guilty, and I've arrested him. To accommodate Superintendent Pruvost, who

120

believes Clodoche to be the murderer, I've also locked up the cripple. Finally, to satisfy M. Malicorne, who believes the guard to be the murderer of Verdinage, I've detained   Jacques Bénard. Each is entitled to his opinion, but mine....'

IX

The clock struck nine.

There was an unusual amount of activity in the Palais de Justice de Compiègne. The magistrates were in a hurry.

In three cars sat Taupinois, Malicorne, Launay, Ernest, Pruvost, Morrow, Lebrument, Chaumel, and—wedged between four inspectors—Chapon, Clodoche, and Bénard.

The procession drove rapidly over the bumpy roads and up the driveway to Marchenoire Manor.

The villagers crowded at the park gate booed when Chapon, Clodoche, and Bénard got out. It took all of Lieutenant Taupinois's authority to prevent them being attacked by the mob before they disappeared inside.

The housemaid-nanny hugged Charles, moaning:

'My poor husband. You didn't do it, did you?... You're innocent!... Tell them you're innocent!'

She uttered a heart-rending cry when she saw the handcuffs on her husband's hands, and had to be restrained.

Gustave, Edmond, and Jeanne, standing together at one end of the hall, looked with pity at the butler and the guard, who had both aged under the strain and looked depressed. The cripple, on the other hand, was smiling stupidly, and appeared oblivious to the gravity of the charges against him.

Adhémar Dupont-Lesguyères was the last to react and greeted magistrates and police officers equally casually.

'How can I be of service, messieurs?' he asked.

'We're going to do a reconstruction of the crime,' replied M. Launay, lighting one of his disgusting cigars. 'The various people present are going to place themselves where they were at the moment they heard the last words of the victim. Everyone of you will act in *exactly* the way you did on the night of October 28... *Exactly*! Bénard here will play the part of the criminal.'

The guard started to protest his innocence, but the magistrate cut him off:

'No one's accusing you of anything, Bénard. For the purposes of the investigation, someone has to play the part of the criminal, and I've decided it will be you.'

The witness made a weary gesture. A night without sleep, punctuated by questioning, had sapped his resistance.

The sinister comedy played out according to the script. Bénard fired a shot from the library entrance. Clodoche knocked on the front door and shouted out. Charles, who had gone to the cellar, came back up. Thérèse came to the door of her room and exchanged a few words with her husband. The butler opened the door to the cripple. Edmond and Gustave, and then Jeanne, descended the staircase.

'That'll be it, for now,' announced the magistrate. 'We'll continue the reconstruction later if need be.'

Me. Lebrument declared:

'Nothing in what we've just seen has established *a priori* my client's guilt. As a consequence, I ask that my client—whose mental retardation renders him incapable of such an act anyway—be released immediately.'

'We haven't finished, Maître!' retorted Pruvost, furious to see his preferred suspect put in the clear.

Tom Morrow observed, in his mellow tones:

'And so, monsieur le juge, as you have so clearly established by the reconstruction we have just witnessed, the murderer *could not have hidden in the cellar with the help of Charles Chapon*, who had time to cross the hallway between the time of the shot and the arrival of Thérèse Chapon.'

'That is indeed what I have established,' replied M. Launay smugly.

Me. Chaumel ventured gently:

'Forgive me, monsieur le juge. If my client had hidden the murderer in the cellar, he could not have helped him get out afterwards, because....'

The magistrate blew out a puff of smoke and gave a growl of displeasure which bemused the timid defence lawyer.

'Maître Chaumel is right,' added the deputy. 'The testimony of the witnesses is categorical. After visiting, or pretending to visit, the cellar, the accused, Charles Chapon, locked the cellar door, and it remained locked until the arrival of the gendarmes.'

'I examined the cellar thoroughly and there was nobody inside,' declared Taupinois.

M. Launay responded sharply:

'Is anyone saying you didn't, lieutenant?'

The officer fell quiet.

Tom Morrow, who had been fiddling with the ribbon of his monocle, asked:

'Would it be possible, monsieur le juge, for me to visit, in your company, this strange cellar from which criminals are able to escape so mysteriously, right under the noses of the police?'

'Willingly!'

The magistrate and Tom Morrow, followed by the deputy, Me. Lebrument, Me.Chaumel, and Adhémar Dupont-Lesguyères, went over to the cellar door.

M. Launay, pointing to the first step of the stairs, explained:

'That is where the accused, Charles Chapon, claims to have discovered the second threatening letter. In my opinion, he never discovered anything. It was he who waited for an opportune moment to place it there, opening the door with a key *to which only he had a copy.*'

'Obviously,' agreed the private detective. 'Charles Chapon could only have found the letter on that step if he himself had placed it there.'

'It's strange, in that case, that my client didn't arrange for someone else to find it, instead of picking it up himself,' observed Me. Chaumel.

M. Launay didn't bother to reply.

The six men descended into the dark, damp cellar.

Tom Morrow roamed around the space, using a torchlight to illuminate the corners that light from the overhead lamp failed to reach.

With an agility surprising in one so corpulent, the private detective ferreted around, sliding between the barrels and kneeling to examine each case of wine.

It was as if he were taking an inventory of the cellar's riches.

One particular wine rack drew his attention, and he shook it as if to test its solidity.

The rack suddenly came loose from the wall and the detective was able to make it pivot like a hinged door. He slid behind it.

'There's a low door!' he exclaimed after a moment of silent research.

'A low door?' repeated the deputy in astonishment. 'A concealed door? Did any of the investigators open it?'

'Well... no....' stammered M. Launay in surprise. 'This is the first time....'

'I never suspected the existence of such a door,' added Adhémar, 'and I'm sure no one else in the manor knew about it.'

'I doubt that,' replied Tom Morrow courteously, as he reappeared covered in dust.

'We have to break it down!' ordered the magistrate, sensing that it might be the key to the mystery.

He called for Edmond Tasseau. The sturdy chauffeur was able to prise the heavy door open, releasing a quick flood of the muddy water that had accumulated behind it, and soaking his trousers.

Without further ado, Tom Morrow plunged into the black hole now revealed, bending down and wriggling on his stomach before finally disappearing.

Several minutes passed whilst the others waited. They were starting to become anxious when a jovial voice shouted:

'Cuckoo! I'm back.'

Tom Morrow, his clothes covered in sticky mud, was standing behind them.

'Well, I'll be blowed!' exclaimed the deputy. 'Where did you come from?'

'I found a sort of passage which was probably part of an old quarry,' explained the detective. 'Everything else underground has collapsed except that section. It comes out in the park, at a spot where there's plenty of undergrowth, near a stone urn to the right of the manor, standing on a mossy plinth.'

Me. Chaumel, perplexed, scratched his chin. This reinforced the magistrate's theory and was damning for his client. It seemed very likely that Verdinage's killer had escaped through this previously unknown passage, and that Charles's complicity was undeniable.

M. Launay appeared vexed by the amateur detective's discovery and could barely disguise his pique. Clearly nothing escaped Tom Morrow's eagle eye.

To soothe the magistrate's feelings, Morrow added:

126

'Luck can play an important role. Sometimes it allows a newcomer to notice something that has escaped the notice of more experienced investigators.'

'But, monsieur, it wasn't luck which prompted you to examine that wine rack so closely,' objected Adhémar Dupont-Lesguyères.

'Almost, monsieur, almost! I first postulated that the letter found on the top step of the cellar stairs had been left there by *someone who hadn't entered by the door*, because the gap underneath the door isn't wide enough to slide a letter through. Therefore, there had to be another way in. It was whilst I was looking for it that I made a trivial observation.'

'And what might that be?' asked Me. Malicorne.

'The metallic wine rack in question held some really old bottles. The ones on the left were *much less dirty than the others*, and some had even had their wax seals broken.'

'True enough,' agreed M. Launay, shrugging his shoulders. 'But what does that prove?'

'Not much, monsieur le juge, except that, on that side, the bottles had been shaken up. That gave me the idea of checking *whether the rack could be move*d. After all, if bottles get shaken, there must be a reason.'

'Your reasoning is sound,' said the magistrate, with a tight-lipped smile.

Trying to keep in his good graces, Tom Morrow continued diplomatically:

'That modest discovery—which you could equally well have made, monsieur le juge—is nothing compared with the most difficult part of the investigation, which you brought to a conclusion with such surprising rapidity. Thanks to you, two accomplices have been arrested and a third will surely follow. Now, those are important results!'

The magistrate refrained from replying.

The secret door was pushed back in place, the rack was moved back in front of it and the six men went back up into the hall.

Tom Morrow looked at his soiled clothes and said solemnly:

'Monsieur le juge, it would not be appropriate for me to stay with you in this condition. I beg leave to wash my hands and face and clean my clothes.'

Gustave Colinet stepped forward and said, in his colourless voice:

'If monsieur will accompany me to M. Verdinage's bathroom, monsieur can wash himself whilst I brush his clothes.'

'I would be very obliged to you,' replied the detective.

He bowed to M. Launay.

'Permit me to be absent for a few moments. I hope I can return in time to hear the conclusions you have drawn from your admirable investigation.'

He straightened up, turned on his muddy heel, and followed Gustave Colinet up the grand staircase.

The magistrate watched him go, and asked himself anxiously whether the amateur detective wasn't subtly mocking him.

THIRD PART

THE AMATEUR DETECTIVE

I

After the departure of the private detective, M. Launay led the deputy, Adhémar, Me. Chaumel, Me. Lebrument and the clerk Ernest into the library.

A large brown stain on the carpet reminded everyone of the dreadful tragedy which had unfolded there.

Feeling a rising anger, the magistrate launched into an outburst:

'Let's be clear! It is I who am in charge of the case, and there is nothing miraculous about the discovery that M. Morrow has just made. It simply confirmed my suspicions. I would have found the secret door through reasoning, rather than by stumbling on clues. I established some time ago that Charles Chapon helped the murderer escape. It now remains for us to unmask the criminal, the criminal whose existence I alone discovered, without the help of a detective fiction fanatic, only good for complicating simple matters.'

'The murderer will end up confessing,' declared M. Malicorne. 'You mark my words!'

'So be it,' conceded M. Launay in exasperation. 'We will give you the satisfaction of interviewing Jacques Bénard one more time.'

He sat down at his desk with his clerk next to him. The deputy, Adhémar, and the two defence lawyers remained standing.

On his orders, Bénard came into the room, led by Pruvost.

'What do you want now?' groused the guard. 'Am I accused, yes or no? Are you going to leave me alone? I protest my arbitrary arrest.'

'Bénard,' replied M. Malicorne calmly, 'what were your movements on the night of the crime?'

'I've already told you twenty times! I was asleep in the guardhouse by the gate. I heard a shot fired up in the manor. I got up and ran to help my master. That's it.'

'Bénard,' said the magistrate, 'you've admitted that the revolver

129

Clodoche found in the fountain belonged to you. It is indisputably the weapon used in the crime, and it bears your fingerprints.'

'So what?'

'You murdered M. Verdinage!'

'That's not true! You're accusing me without proof. I refuse to reply. I want a lawyer!'

The deputy banged his fist on the table.

'Don't deny it!' he shouted. 'You're the murderer. You're the famous stranger who appeared at the park gate on the night of October 28. It was you! It could only have been you! You carefully hid your face and avoided speaking to Clodoche, *for fear of him recognising you!*'

'So you say.'

'A further proof: witnesses say that the dogs started to bark, but fell silent almost immediately. They did so because they sniffed you out. They did so because they were used to you.'

'It's all theory. Just suppositions, nothing more.'

'It was you who did it. You killed Verdinage using your revolver. And your accomplice Charles helped you escape.'

'Charles?' repeated the guard in astonishment.

'Yes, Charles. Charles Chapon. He locked the cellar door so that you had time to move the wine rack and escape through the underground passage.'

'What underground passage?'

'Don't play the imbecile. You know very well what I'm talking about. Everything is clear now. Even your late arrival, because you had to go back to the guardhouse to get out of your mud-covered clothes before turning up at the manor.'

'I didn't change my clothes!'

'And you tossed the revolver into the fountain on the way.'

'And what else?'

'Bénard, everything points to your guilt. There's no point in denying it. That will only annoy the court and lead to the maximum sentence. Your goose is cooked! What's the point in continuing your ridiculous defence? Confess and save yourself.'

'I'm telling you it wasn't me!'

The magistrate made a gesture of impatience:

'Very well,' he growled. 'Take him away.'

The superintendent grabbed the guard's arm and escorted him out of the room.

M. Launay, his face purple with anger, crushed his cigar out in a saucer, got to his feet, and shouted:

'That imbecile insists on denying the evidence.'

'I told you so!' said the deputy triumphantly.

'In fact, all we have against him is some serious presumptions,' said Pruvost. 'What we need is proof.'

The deputy raised his arms to the ceiling.

'Proof! Proof!'

'Nothing could be easier,' said a voice.

Tom Morrow, who had just tiptoed into the room, added:

'There is, in fact, a way to prove that Bénard was not asleep in the guardhouse at the time of the crime.'

'Oh, really?' replied M. Launay cynically.

'With your permission, we will conduct a small experiment. Bénard's revolver is in your possession, is it not, monsieur le juge?'

'Here it is,' said the clerk, putting the weapon on the desk.

'Would you hand it to M. Dupont-Lesguyères, please?... Perfect! Now, with your agreement, monsieur le juge, we will take Bénard back to the guardhouse, and when M. Dupont-Lesguyères sees him go in, he will close the front door, stand in front of the library door, and fire a bullet into the ceiling.'

M. Launay looked at the private detective. Deciding that the fellow was serious, he turned to address Verdinage's secretary:

'Please do exactly what M. Morrow says.'

The magistrate, the deputy, Tom Morrow, Me. Lebrument, Me. Chaumel, Bénard, and the superintendent traipsed down to the guardhouse.

They returned a quarter of an hour later and M. Launay, a new cigar dangling from his lips, addressed Adhémar impatiently:

'Why didn't you follow my orders, monsieur?'

'But I did, monsieur le juge,' protested the other in astonishment. 'I did exactly what you told me to do.'

The young secretary indicated the presence of the bullet in the ceiling above.

'We didn't hear anything,' replied the magistrate incredulously.

The private detective intervened:

131

'We didn't hear anything, monsieur le juge, because—just as I thought—it's impossible to hear a shot from that distance if the front door is closed, and the shot is fired in the hall in front of the library.'

He turned to face the guard:

'Isn't that so, Bénard?'

The latter went pale and turned his head away.

'If, on the night of the crime, you did indeed hear the shot, it means that you must have been near the house,' continued the private detective, giving the guard a steely gaze.

'It's true,' admitted Bénard in a low voice.

M. Launay felt he had to continue such a promising line of inquiry.

'Why did you lie by pretending you were asleep in your bed when the murder was taking place?' he asked.

'Because I'd already told the gendarmes, and it was too late to take it back.'

'So why did you lie to the gendarmes?'

'Because then I would have to have admitted I was outside.'

'So?'

'So, then they would have asked what I was doing, and I didn't want to tell them that I, the guard....'

''Go on. Tell me, what were you doing?'

'I was laying down traps in the park.'

The magistrate coughed incredulously, and continued:

'Then where exactly were you at the time of the crime?'

'I was behind the house. When I heard the dogs I dropped the traps and approached the right side of the manor.'

'The right side. Go on.'

'I could see a light shining at the gate.'

'Clodoche's lantern.'

'I heard footsteps and saw the light coming up the driveway. I hid behind the stone urn.'

'Behind the stone urn. Better and better!'

'I recognised Clodoche's footsteps as he was limping alongside another man whose features were hidden in the darkness. When they got close to the house, I hid myself carefully. When I next looked, they had arrived at the front steps, which I couldn't see from my hiding-place. All I could see was the light from the lantern that Clodoche must have placed on the top step.'

132

'That's correct. What did you hear next?

'A detonation, which must have come from inside the house, then Clodoche's shouts as he tried to open the door.'

'If someone had tried to escape through the door, would you have seen them?'

'Certainly, because I remained there, watching, whilst the door was opened for the cripple and shut behind him.'

'So far, your testimony agrees with all the other witnesses.'

'It agrees too well!' retorted the deputy.

The guard insisted:

'I've told the truth.'

'You're lying,' replied M. Malicorne brutally. 'You're lying! You've lied since your first questioning. And you continue to lie.'

'Monsieur le....'

'Shut up!'

M. Launay, Adhémar Dupont-Lesguyères, Tom Morrow, the two defence lawyers, the superintendent, and the clerk wondered why the deputy accused the man, whose testimony had seemed so sincere, of lying.

Finally showing his hand, M. Malicorne pointed an accusing finger at Bénard:

'I say you're lying, and I can prove it!' he shouted. 'You claim that, whilst Verdinage was being murdered, you were hiding behind the stone urn to the right of the manor. But, two steps away from there, the underground passage that we... that monsieur le juge discovered comes out.'

'What underground passage?'

'Don't play the innocent! You know very well that there's an underground passage which leads from the cellar to the outside.'

'An underground passage! Well, there's a thing.'

'The aforementioned passage, which begins behind a wine rack, comes out just behind the stone urn, close to the spot where you claim you were hiding. Now, I can confirm that the murderer left the cellar (where his accomplice Charles Chapon had allowed him to hide) via that passage.

'Therefore, if you were indeed hiding behind the urn, you would have seen the murderer emerge from the undergrowth.'

'I never saw anything more than what I've already told you, and I never knew anything about an underground passage.'

'Let me remind you, Bénard, that the murder weapon is *your* revolver, and that the only fingerprints on the butt are yours!'

'And Clodoche's!' added the superintendent.

'That's true,' agreed the deputy, 'but it's quite natural that his fingerprints are to be found on the revolver he discovered. But *the presence of Bénard's are much more difficult to explain.'*

'It's not true!' protested the guard. 'I'm a poacher, not a murderer!'

'Let me remind you, Bénard,' continued M. Malicorne, 'that, of all the people currently inhabiting the manor, *you were the only one present* when Desrousseaux was murdered. I would also remind you that you were the *only* servant—except for M. Dupont-Lesguyères, whom I'm not worried about—not to be on the scene of the crime when Verdinage was murdered. And, finally, let me remind you that *nobody was as obstinate as you* in urging the victim to leave *the forbidden house.'*

'I preferred Marchenoire to remain empty so that I could continue poaching undisturbed... and the threatening letters really did worry me, because I liked M. Verdinage very much.'

'A feeling he did not reciprocate, because he was ready to sack you: the way in which you exploited Clodoche's misery and weakness disgusted him.'

'So you say.'

'Bénard,' interjected M. Launay, 'I'm arresting you for the intentional homicide of M. Verdinage... Pruvost, handcuff him... We will immediately search the guardhouse.'

Bénard was led down to the small building.

Under his nose, the superintendent and two inspectors rummaged thoroughly through the two rooms.

The furniture consisted of a bed for Bénard, a straw mattress for Clodoche, a wardrobe, and a rickety table. The inspectors were on the point of leaving, having found nothing, when Tom Morrow suggested examining a woodshed leaning against the building.

The police took his advice and, to his great satisfaction, Pruvost found an old typewriter buried under a pile of logs.

'Is this the machine you used to type the famous threatening letters?' asked the magistrate.

Bénard replied in an emotionless voice.

'That machine isn't mine... I don't even know how to use one.'

'Are you going to tell me that Clodoche used it to write love letters to his girl friends?' sneered M. Launay. He stopped joking and said harshly:

'Bénard, don't push my patience to its limits. Faced with such evidence, at least have the courage to confess.'

The guard responded simply:

'I'm innocent of the murder of M. Verdinage.'

Annoyed, the magistrate made a sign to the inspectors and ordered:

'Take him away!'

Bénard left in the company of four safe hands.

'Well,' said M. Launay, taking Tom Morrow's arm, 'you wanted to see how I ended my investigations. I hope you're fully satisfied.'

'I've been delighted to see it,' replied the detective, 'but please allow me to voice one last tiny objection, monsieur le juge.'

'Go ahead,' declared the magistrate confidently.

'Well, if Bénard is declared to be the murderer, as you have so clearly done, it will be troublesome... very troublesome.'

'For him?' laughed M. Launay.

'No, for you, monsieur le juge.'

'And why is that?' asked the magistrate in astonishment.

'Why, monsieur le juge, because once the crime was committed, he had to have left the manor in order to be at the front door for the other servants, assembled in the hall, to let him in.'

'But, of course, mon cher monsieur, it's as clear as crystal. After having killed his victim, the guard left the manor.'

'That's precisely what is very troublesome for you, monsieur le juge... *because Bénard could not have left the manor.*'

'You must be pulling my leg! We know that the murderer escaped through the cellar and the underground passage.'

'I'm truly sorry to contradict you, monsieur le juge, but *the murderer cannot logically have escaped that way.* It's impossible. Completely impossible!'

II

M. Launay was so taken aback for the moment that his eyes widened and his mouth fell open.

Two contradictory thoughts occurred to him: either Tom Morrow was mad, or—even worse!—the amateur detective was mocking him, the official representative of law and order.

Yet, when he claimed that Verdinage's murderer could not have escaped through the underground passage, he appeared neither demented nor frivolous.

Tom Morrow had gone down to the fountain, where the magistrate joined him and pressed him to explain his mysterious utterances.

The detective replied affably that he needed to cast his mind back to the *precise moment* when, following the magistrate's own order, the chauffeur Tasseau opened the low door that had just been discovered behind the wine rack.

'All I remember,' replied the magistrate, 'is that he had great difficulty pushing it open, because the hinges were rusty.'

'Great difficulty indeed, monsieur le juge, but don't you think there could have been another reason?'

'What?'

'For example, because there was *a heavy weight pushing back from the other side.*'

'I don't follow you,' replied the magistrate brusquely.

'Forgive me, monsieur le juge, I'm not explaining myself well,' said the private detective. 'Let me be more specific.'

'Very well, but for heaven's sake, be brief.'

'Why, the weight of the water inside the underground passage, monsieur le juge.'

'That's right,' M. Launay conceded, 'because Tasseau was drenched when he eventually managed to push the door open. But that doesn't explain why....'

'I'm getting there, monsieur le juge, but first may I remind you that it was raining on the night of the crime, and had rained incessantly all the days of the preceding week.'

'I'll grant you that,' replied the magistrate, 'but what has that got to do with anything?'

'Because, monsieur le juge, once the door was opened the cellar was flooded, and, because the floor was made of concrete, the water could not dissipate as quickly as it had arrived.'

'That's obvious.... But the murderer....?'

'If the murderer had previously opened the door to escape, monsieur le juge, there would already have been water on the impermeable floor when we arrived. Needless to say, your perspicacity will lead you to conclude that, *for at least a week before the crime was committed, the secret door could not have been opened.*

'Therefore, monsieur le juge, you are forced to admit that Verdinage's murderer, whomsoever he may be, *could not have used the underground passage to escape from the forbidden house.*'

Faced with the irrefutable logic, M. Launay was forced to concede that his entire case had suddenly collapsed.

If Bénard, despite the complicity of Charles Capon, could not have escaped from the cellar via the underground passage, how could he have left the manor after committing his foul deed?

Tom Morrow, eyes down, appeared to be contemplating his fine shoes, to which some sticky mud was still attached.

The magistrate finally understood that, behind the foppish exterior, lurked a first-class criminologist, whom he had been wrong to view with contempt.

He decided that it was preferable to work closely with the private detective and claim all the credit afterwards. Such an inelegant approach was a blow to his self-esteem but, in the end, it was the result that counted.

It was therefore in a much gentler tone that he now asked:

'Well, Monsieur Morrow?'

'Well, monsieur le juge?' replied the private detective, in the same tone.

M. Launay realised that, having shown him he was on the wrong path, Tom Morrow was in no hurry to show him the right one.

Bottling up his rage, and making an effort which wounded his vanity, he asked:

'So, according to you, my dear colleague, Bénard and Charles Chapon were wrongly charged?'

'Who knows?' replied Tom Morrow, with the affability which so grated on the magistrate's nerves. He realised that, henceforth, he would have to drag information out of the other, like pulling teeth—information which he had previously disdained.

He decided to speculate out loud and observe the private detective's reactions to his hypotheses.

'Could it be that Bénard and Chapon are not guilty?'

Tom Morrow remained impassive.

'Or that one of them is innocent?'

Again, no response.

'Or that Clodoche, who led the visitor to Verdinage, let him escape?'

Tom Morrow remained silent.

The magistrate turned to face the private detective:

'Surely you must have an opinion about the business at hand?'

Tom Morrow made a vague gesture.

M. Launay continued, refusing to give up hope of overcoming the private detective's stubbornness.

'Who could the murderer be?'

He walked slowly back to the manor, followed by his colleague.

'Who could the murderer be?' repeated the private detective in a low voice as they were crossing the hallway.

He stopped in surprise at the library doorway. Lieutenant Taupinois was holding Adhémar against the stone mantelpiece.

Looking haggard, the secretary's head was turned to avoid the officer's penetrating gaze.

So, he continued to suspect the young Marquis Dupont-Lesguyères of being Verdinage's murder!

Lieutenant Taupinois declared, without taking his eyes off the secretary:

'It's easy to reconstruct the crime because of the numerous depositions whose accuracy is not in doubt, so we know the movements of everyone who was in the manor on the fatal night.'

He paused and added:

'There's only one person whose movements remain unknown, and that person *is you!*'

'Lieutenant Taupinois is right,' said M. Launay, stepping forward.

Adhémar Dupont-Lesguyères was visibly shaken and went pale. His torture was about to commence!

After a week of investigation, the magistrate was back where he started and, humiliatingly, had to admit that the gendarme's assertion was not without merit.

'Yes,' continued the magistrate, 'it's the truth. You said you had permission to spend the night outside. But what weight can I attach to your testimony if no one can confirm it?'

'But,' stammered the young man, 'I went to the village ball... I was dancing... Plenty of people saw me... There are witnesses.'

'So there were,' mocked M. Launay. 'But you left the ball at midnight, contrary to your testimony, which was false on many points. And you've given no information about your movements after that time.'

Adhémar Dupont-Lesguyères seemed to   lose his mind. He mumbled:

'I was... I was... I don't remember... I was drunk.'

'That's ridiculous!' sneered the magistrate. 'Your alibi is nonexistent. I knew I wasn't mistaken.'

'Monsieur le juge....'

'Furthermore, your past weighs against you. You wrote a cheque which bounced.'

'There were no charges. My family paid the bill.'

'It doesn't matter. The fact is there. You're a delinquent. For an entire year, you sponged off a poor young girl. Your father cut off your allowance. To survive, you entered Verdinage's service, but instead of rehabilitating yourself through honest work, you murdered your employer in order to rob him.'

'No! No! I swear....'

The magistrate took a puff on his disgusting cigar:

'Who supervised the renovation of the manor before Verdinage moved in?'

'It was I, monsieur le juge, but....'

'How could you have not known about the underground passage? You kept silent about your discovery, planning to use it for your criminal ends.'

'It's not true! I didn't know about it! How could I have....'

'And then, Monsieur Dupont-Lesguyères, there are the threatening letters... *The three letters Verdinage received were all typed.*'

'Yes, monsieur le juge, but they found the typewriter in Bénard's log pile.'

'Planted! Planted in order to put me off the scent. *You are the only one here who knows how to use a typewriter properly*, which is a curious coincidence which needs further examination.'

Adhémar's shoulders slumped and he began to shake.

M. Launay continued implacably:

'Adhémar Dupont-Lesguyères, what were your movements between the hours of midnight and five o'clock in the morning during the night of October 28 and 29?'

'I don't know! I don't know!' sobbed the young secretary.

The magistrate declared:

'I'll give you five minutes to produce a satisfactory response. If not....'

With that threat hanging over the Adonis's head, he waited, eyes glued to his wrist watch.

Seconds, then minutes passed.

A painful silence descended on the room.

Adhémar, his eyes glazed and his lips pinched, straightened up.

Suddenly the magistrate announced:

'Adhémar Dupont-Lesguyères, I hereby charge you with the murder of Napoléon Verdinage.'

The young secretary, haggard and trembling, got to his feet:

'I swear I'm not a murderer!' he exclaimed with some effort.

M. Launay shrugged his shoulders and replied:

'Easy enough to say, but you have to prove it... And that's more difficult.'

III

Tom Morrow entered the library.

'And that makes four!' he cried joyfully.

'What do you mean?' growled the magistrate.

'I mean that, after arresting Clodoche, Charles Chapon, and Jacques Bénard, you're going to inflict the same fate on this young man. That means that half of Verdinage's staff is now under lock and key. I can't imagine you're going to stop there, and it won't be long before you've added Edmond and Jeanne Tasseau, Thérèse Chapon, and Gustave Colinet to your collection.'

The magistrate retorted sharply:

'I may just do that, if it's useful.'

'And that might be the smart thing to do,' continued Tom Morrow offhandedly.'That way you will have all the witnesses to the tragedy.'

'Exactly!'

'But can you be sure you've detained the man who entered the manor on the night of October 28... the man who entered and was unable to leave?'

Disconcerted, M. Launay remained quiet.

Tom Morrow went over to Adhémar.

'M. Dupont-Lesguyères,' he said, 'I'm going to invite you to confess.'

The young secretary hung his head.

'M. Dupont-Lesguyères,' persisted the private detective, 'if you insist on remaining silent, I shall be obliged to answer on your behalf.'

Adhémar shot him a grief-stricken look.

Tom Morrow turned to address M. Launay:

'I would like to establish the movements of the newly-charged suspect during the night of the crime.'

'That's impossible, because Dupont-Lesguyères refuses to talk,' growled the magistrate.

'His silence is immaterial,' replied the private detective, 'because there's not a single one of his movements that I don't know about.'

M. Launay gasped in astonishment:

'You know everything?'

'I know only that, upon leaving the café *Ménard jeune*, M. Dupont- Lesguyères went to the *Coup de Fusil* auberge.'

Adhémar's shocked reaction confirmed that the detective was telling the truth.

Tom Morrow continued:

'How do I know that? I was on an assignment. A very honourable Parisian family, whom I shall not name, charged me with finding a young girl who had run away. I was lucky enough to find her in a Montmartre dance hall of ill repute and take her promptly back to her parents. My enquiries led me to shadow one Emile Blin, known as "Milo-le-Frisé," a small-time criminal who dabbled in many kinds of nefarious activity, including selling cocaine. Eventually I tailed him to the *Coup de Fusil,* which he frequented twice a month in order to sell packets of the white powder to clients of the region, including a certain Adhémar Dupont-Lesguyères.'

The secretary's eyes widened as he wondered how the policeman could know so much.

Tom Morrow continued:

'I must add that I wasn't alone when I visited the *Coup de Fusil*. I had alerted an old friend of mine, Inspector Savinien, who had recently been assigned to track drug-smuggling. I told him I was shadowing "Milo-le-Frisé," and he asked to accompany me in order to catch the criminal in the act. Don't you remember seeing me there, M. Dupont-Lesguyères?'

The Adonis shook his head.

'Don't you remember a drunken Englishman who murdered our language every time he opened his mouth, sitting at the table next to where you were drinking with "Milo-le-Frisé"?'

'Was that you?' murmured Adhémar.

'It was indeed. I had adopted that camouflage in order not to arouse suspicion, and it obviously worked.'

M. Launay remarked impatiently:

'That's all very well, M. Morrow, but what does that have to do with Verdinage's murder?'

'The question of timing,' replied the private detective. 'After the arrest of "Milo-le-Frisé," I went back to the hotel room I had booked in Compiègne. When I woke up, I learnt that a crime had been committed at Marchenoire Manor. Whilst I was assisting Savinien, an unknown visitor had mysteriously killed the lord of the manor. In the course of my frequent visits to the *Coup de Fusil* I had learnt the history of *the forbidden house*, but had attributed the stories to village gossip. Verdinage's murder changed all that. Such a mysterious crime intrigued me.'

He ran his short fingers through his long hair and continued:

'My first surprise was when I saw the photograph of the victim's private secretary, "Milo-le-Frisé's" client, in the newspaper. I had intended to notify the gendarmerie of the young man's unbreakable alibi, when you took charge of the case, monsieur le juge. Now that M. Dupont-Lesguyère's innocence has once again been called into question, I felt obliged to tell what I know, despite your new arrest's objections.'

Without a word, the Adonis pulled a small sachet out of his pocket and, with a trembling hand, gave it to the magistrate.

As M. Launay was taking it, Tom Morrow added:

'This is a sign that the young man renounces his foolish ways. Inspector Savinien has promised to keep an eye on him, and I recommend he be dismissed forthwith.'

Anxious not to upset the private detective, on whom he was likely to depend in solving the case, the magistrate reluctantly agreed:

'You are free to go, monsieur. Please leave!'

As the young Adonis left, after fervently thanking Tom Morrow, M.Launay shook his head in exasperation.

He had to face the fact that he had failed miserably. All his assumptions had proved to be wrong. How sure he had been as he clapped Clodoche and Charles Chapon in irons, how certain of himself when he condemned Jacques Bénard to the same fate. And now he was going to have to release them all, just as he had released Adhémar.

And now he was going to swallow his pride and ask Tom Morrow for help.

Trembling with rage, M. Launay shouted:

'So, monsieur, if Verdinage's murderer is not Adhémar Dupont-Lesguyères, or Clodoche, or Charles Chapon, or Jacques Bénard, who is it? And how did he escape from *the forbidden house?*'

The private detective played with the ribbon of his monocle for a moment, then replied:

'I have never pretended, monsieur le juge, that I knew who the culprit was. I only made some simple assumptions. I would never assert, before a magistrate of your standing....'

'Nevertheless, M. Morrow, my dear colleague, I would like...because I have not entirely succeeded... in unravelling completely this damned puzzle....'

'I feel sure, monsieur le juge, that a man of your perspicacity must eventually....'

'No, M. Morrow. You know perfectly well that I won't find anything... I confess: I am completely lost... I beg you to give me your advice.'

The amateur policeman took pity on the magistrate who was humiliating himself so pitifully, and replied gently:

'In my humble opinion, monsieur le juge, there's only one logical solution.'

'Suicide!' exclaimed M. Launay.

'No, monsieur le juge, if it had been suicide, there would have been gunpowder around the wound, as Lieutenant Taupinois observed at the start of the investigation. Furthermore, the medical examiner stated that the murderer fired from several metres away from the victim, probably from the doorway of the library.'

Choosing his words carefully, Tom Morrow declared:

'Because you have done me the honour of asking my opinion, monsieur le juge, I shall take the liberty of submitting *the hypothesis which explains everything.*'

IV

The library door opened.

The deputy entered, accompanied by Me. Lebrument, Me. Chaumel and the superintendent.

'There has been no proof of the charges brought against my client,' declared Clodoche's lawyer. 'He has never wavered in his testimony.'

'The same is true for my client,' echoed Chapon's lawyer.

'Messieurs,' replied the magistrate nervously, 'my investigation has just taken a step forward. I have discovered....'

Seeing the calm look in the amateur policeman's eye, he corrected himself:

'We have just discovered that your clients did not help the murderer escape, at least not through the underground passage.'

'In that case,' chimed Me. Chaumel and Me. Lebrument in unison, 'my client must immediately be released.'

'Obviously,' conceded M. Launay with bad grace, because he had to admit that no plausible charges could now be brought against the accused. 'Obviously... Clodoche, who had introduced the nocturnal visitor to Marchenoire and who, at the time of the crime, was seen on the front steps by the valet Gustave Colinet, could not have committed the crime... Jacques Bénard, who showed up at the front door after the servants had discovered the body, could not have committed the murder because it has been established that the murderer could not have got out of the residence... Adhémar Dupont-Lesguyères is innocent for other reasons... In truth, I only charged—or failed to charge—Clodoche, Bénard and Dupont-Lesguyères under pressure from M. Pruvost, M. Malicorne and Lieutenant Taupinois. Personally, I never believed in their guilt.'

He took his time lighting a cigar and continued:

'That leaves Charles Chapon... The main beneficiary of Verdinage's will, but on the way to being disinherited, he was the only one with a motive for killing his master. Plus which, he behaved strangely on the night of the crime... Let us not forget that he left the conjugal bedroom surreptitiously and was found, only a few seconds after the fatal shot, in the hall, in front of the cellar door, only a short distance from the library.'

'If you please!' protested Me. Chaumel. 'Even the gravest assumptions cannot prevail over precise facts. This affair is, at the same time, very simple and very complex. It can be summarised in four words, heavy with mystery: *a man came in.*'

The young lawyer was making grand gestures, as if he were entering a plea.

'A man came in, led by Clodoche... A witness saw him traverse the park... That man entered the manor and was unable to leave... That man had come to Marchenoire with the intention of killing Verdinage... That man is indisputably the author of the threatening letters... Of all the threatening letters... the same spelling error found in each of the epistles, proving that there was only one author... That man, who arrived promptly at the sinister rendezvous, executed his criminal threat... That man alone can and must be suspected... Who is that man?'

Superintendent Pruvost replied:

'I never claimed that Clodoche was the guilty party. I simply think that it's curious that he was unable to see the features of the person he brought in here on the night of October 28. I continue to believe that he was an accomplice.'

Me. Lebrument intervened:

'That's your right,' he declared, 'but I remember that there was a violent storm over the whole region that night. And I recall that neither Gustave Colinet, watching from the window of his room, nor Jacques Bénard, crouching behind a stone urn, could discern the visitor's features either.'

The deputy, who had refrained from comment thus far, spoke up.

'I believe Jacques Bénard's deposition should be taken with a grain of salt,' he said. 'Out of all of the inhabitants of the manor, the guard is the only one who is logically a suspect. This uncouth individual possesses none of the characteristics that would restrain a homicidal impulse: not the education of Dupont-Lesguyères, nor the docility of Clodoche, nor the devotion of Charles Chapon. Bénard considered Marchenoire to be his own personal property, and those who tried to buy it as intruders. Of all those mixed up in this crime, he was the only one present when one of Verdinage's predecessors died in a manner that was believed to be accidental. The murder weapon is his and his fingerprints are on it.'

'As are those of Clodoche!' interjected the superintendent, determined not to admit the cripple's innocence.

'As are those of Clodoche, who retrieved the revolver from the fountain,' continued M. Malicorne. 'Finally, a typewriter was found in the woodshed adjacent to the guardhouse, and the three anonymous letters were typed.'

Pruvost declared ironically:

'It remains to be seen whether that machine was used to type the letters and who used it.'

'With monsieur le juge's permission, I will look into that,' replied Tom Morrow.

'Permission granted,' agreed M. Launay. 'I doubt, however, that Bénard knows how to use such a machine. Even if he does, it would be only too easy to deny it.'

'That's why I've no intention of asking him,' replied the detective. 'All I ask is that the machine be brought here.'

'Willingly!'

So saying, Pruvost left the room and returned shortly with the suspect machine.

At Tom Morrow's request, the clerk Ernest handed over the three thin sheets of onion paper.

The policeman addressed Adhémar:

'Of all the people in the room,' he said, 'you are the only one who cannot claim he does not know how to use such a machine, because that forms part of your official duties.'

'That's true,' replied the other, turning white with the fear that such an admission would cause additional suspicion to fall on him.

'You will therefore re-type, in front of us and as exactly as possible, the three letters.'

The typewriter clattered under the young man's agile fingers. He handed over a sheet of paper on which he had reproduced the texts of the three missives.

'Perfect!' exclaimed the detective. 'You have followed the same spacing and line length. I notice right away that your duplicates are exactly like the originals.'

Pruvost sneered:

'What's surprising about that? All the typewriters in the same series produce the same results.'

'Not exactly,' retorted Tom Morrow with a smile. 'There are always almost imperceptible faults, for example slight differences in the heights of capital letters, or a slightly shorter crossbar for the letter "t." These characteristics appear in the letters Verdinage received, and also in those M. Dupont-Lesguyères just typed. From which I conclude that the anonymous letters were indeed typed on this machine. And now, monsieur le juge, will you please call Bénard?'

The guard came in, accompanied by two burly inspectors.

'Now what?' he growled. 'Isn't it over yet? I tell you I'm innocent. What more do you want?'

The amateur policeman pointed to the typewriter and asked:

'Do you recognise this instrument?'

'No... no....'

'You're very forgetful, Bénard, because it was found in the shed next to your dwelling.'

'I know, but I don't know who put it there. It was done out of spite.'

'Do you know what purpose it serves?'

'Of course. I saw M. Dupont-Lesguyères use it several times in M. Verdinage's office. I even saw other....'

He stopped, as if he had said too much.

'You saw other owners of Marchenoire use similar machines?'

'That's it.'

'There's nothing wrong with that, Bénard. The banker Abraham Goldenberg had one, I'm sure.'

'The banker Abraham Goldenberg?'

Sensing a trap, the guard looked panic-stricken.

'What's so surprising about that?' continued Tom Morrow. 'He probably had several. One of them might easily have disappeared when he left. In fact, the one found in the woodshed is five years old. Isn't that about the time when Abraham Goldenberg went to jail?'

'I... I don't know.'

The policeman waited several moments before asking:

'Do you know how to type?'

'Of course not.'

'But you've been to school?'

150

'Of course, but they didn't teach that.'

'What did you learn?'

'Reading and writing, but with a pen, like everyone.'

'Sit down at that desk. Take a sheet of paper and a pen and write what I dictate.'

The guard reluctantly obeyed.

Pacing up and down, Tom Morrow dictated:

'*I... Bénard... Jacques...* Comma...*am innocent of the murder of M. Verdinage...* Comma... *my master.* Full stop. New line.

'*Because I was in the park...* Comma... *at the time of the crime...* Are you following me?'

'Yes, monsieur.'

'So, let us continue... *at the time of the crime...* Comma... *All suspicion is forbidden to Justice.*'

'*... to Justice,*' repeated the guard.

'Sign and give me the paper.'

The guard obeyed and handed the written page over.

'What a pity,' observed Tom Morrow after reading it, 'that you weren't taught to spell.'

'Now what?' growled the guard. 'What does spelling have to do with M. Verdinage's murder?'

'Quite a lot, as it happens, Bénard. See for yourself. You've written "forbidden" as "forbiddin," just like the writer of the anonymous letters!'

Bénard knew his goose was cooked. Nevertheless, he persisted stubbornly.

'I'm innocent! I'm innocent!'

The magistrate ordered him removed from the room and turned to André Pruvost.

'The culprit has been revealed,' he said. 'Despite his protests, we can now be certain that it was he who murdered Verdinage.'

Affably, Tom Morrow intervened once again:

'*I'm afraid you're mistaken, monsieur le juge.*'

V

Satisfied with the consternation his reply had caused, Tom Morrow continued:

'Each to his own opinion, monsieur le juge, but if Bénard killed Verdinage, I can't explain how, after the act, he managed to leave *the forbidden house.*'

'But....'

'Because we know the guard was outside when the crime was discovered by the servant. Now, Bénard could not have escaped through the shuttered windows, nor by the front door, blocked by Clodoche and under surveillance by Gustave Colinet, nor by the underground passage whose door was not opened during the night of the crime.'

'Nevertheless,' protested M. Malicorne haughtily, 'Bénard was the author of the three anonymous letters!'

'Did I say anything to the contrary?'

'You said....'

'That Bénard was not the murderer. That's not the same thing.'

Tom Morrow sat down casually in front of M. Launay.

'Before that interlude,' he said, addressing the magistrate in particular, 'I was about to present a hypothesis, *the only hypothesis which explains everything.*'

'That's right,' said the latter, 'and I must confess that I'm eager to know your thoughts about the tragedy of Marchenoire and that nocturnal visitor who entered the manor and then disappeared without trace.'

'Before that,' continued the private detective, 'I want you to know that I am convinced that the typewriter found in the woodshed belonged to Bénard, and that the crafty fellow was the author of all the threatening letters written to frighten successive occupants of the manor. And the ruse worked because, when they left, he became the veritable master of Marchenoire and was able to continue his poaching undisturbed.

'But Verdinage, more courageous or more stubborn than the

153

others, refused to leave *the forbidden house*. Bénard pretended to believe that the threat was very real, and pressed him to leave.

'Incidentally, I believe that the second occupant of the manor, the late Desrousseaux, was accidentally killed by one of Bénard's fellow poachers.

'Nevertheless, Bénard continued to set his traps and made quite a profit selling hares to the *Coup de Fusil*. This was told to me confidentially, following the arrest of "Milo-le-Frisé."

'So, Bénard typed his threatening letters on the machine to avoid being incriminated by his handwriting, not realising that a spelling error would betray him.

'Bénard had lived on the property for too long not to have known about the underground passage, and made use of it to place the *second* threatening letter on the cellar steps. The passage was still passable because the heavy rains had not yet begun.

'He had simply placed the first letter on the library mantelpiece whilst Me. Laridoire was showing M. Verdinage around the manor.

'And, even more simply, he had posted the *third* letter in the hope of frightening his master into finally leaving.

'On the night of the crime, Bénard was out poaching. He was sure that his master would not be out in the park after having received that last letter.

'Bénard heard the dogs barking and approached the manor to see what was happening.

'Unaware of Clodoche's assignment, he was surprised to see the cripple, lantern in hand, leading a stranger towards the manor.

'Let us not dwell on that episode, which is covered by the guard's second deposition. Suffice to say that Bénard was two steps away from the exit from the underground passage, of which he was well aware. He would certainly have seen the mysterious murderer *if he had attempted to escape that way*. What's more, as we have shown, the concealed doorway *could not have been in use that night*.

'In addition, the miscreant could not have left by the front door, because the driveway was illuminated for most of its length by the lantern Clodoche had placed on the steps.

'And that also rules out any complicity by Clodoche, should one try to claim that he helped his master's murderer to escape.

'Gustave Colinet, who was watching out of his bedroom

window, has already testified that he saw no one leave by the front door.

'We can therefore conclude that no one left *the forbidden house*, and that therefore *the murderer remained inside.*

'Where did he hide?

'He could not have hidden in one of the rooms of the ground floor, nor any of the rooms upstairs, nor the cellar.'

'So?'

'So, the murderer wasn't hidden at all. *He was in the hall, where everyone could see him.*

'I don't mean that all Verdinage's servants were complicit. No, *the murderer acted without an accomplice.*

'I can prove that easily. Let us go back to the crime itself and recall the atmosphere of panic that reigned after Charles Chapon discovered the second letter, placed on the cellar steps by Bénard.

'Now let us suppose that someone, having, in the course of his duties, discovered the entrance to the underground passage and Bénard's little scheme, decided to *exploit* the general anxiety by blaming a fictitious person for the murder he was planning to commit .

'That person learns of the arrival of the third letter, the one containing the death warrant. In fact, he already knows that Bénard sends them at monthly intervals.

'All he needs to do is murder Verdinage for the crime to be *attributed to the mysterious letter-writer* who announced:

TONIGHT, AT AROUND MIDNIGHT, I WILL COME TO MARCHENOIRE MANOR AND I WILL KILL YOU.

'So let us look at *who* had an interest in killing the lord of the manor. Let us look for someone who would profit.'

'*Charles Chapon, the butler!*' exclaimed the magistrate.

'It is, in fact, Charles Chapon,' agreed Tom Morrow. 'The butler, together with his wife, is the principal beneficiary of his master's will.

'Threatened with disinheritance because of his drinking, Charles Chapon decides to murder Verdinage in order to protect the large fortune coming to him.

'Better still, circumstances dictate October 28 to be the date of the murder.

155

'Thérèse Chapon had noticed M. Dupont-Lesguyères's unease as he returned from the limousine ride, and concluded that the third letter had arrived on the expected date: one month after the second letter. She was sincerely very attached to her master, and her grief at his death was genuinely touching.

'It is inconceivable, surely, that she did not look for the letter and did indeed find it in a drawer. It is equally inconceivable that she would keep the secret to herself. She, quite naturally, confided in her husband.

'Charles Chapon, then, knew that the third letter had arrived and knew of its contents. The moment had come for him to act.

'When Thérèse woke up on the night of the crime, she was alone in their room. The butler had left silently as soon as she had fallen asleep and before Verdinage came down to the library.

'Making a detour, his face hidden behind the upturned collar of his coat and his hat jammed down over his eyes, Charles waited at the park gate.

'His crime was premeditated. The scoundrel must have thought about it for quite some time. His duties allowed him to spy on his master constantly.

'Which is probably how he came to learn about Clodoche's assignment. He had the diabolical idea of playing the role of the visitor Verdinage was expecting. He knew, better than anyone, that the visitor would not come, because he did not exist, having been created out of thin air by the guard.

'Charles followed Clodoche up to the manor. He avoided speaking for fear of his voice being recognised. You know the rest.

'Verdinage welcomed the visitor with the words that he had already rehearsed in his head: "No! I won't leave!"

'Charles Chapon, by way of response, pointed the revolver at his master, who recoiled into the library....

'Charles Chapon shot Verdinage, who collapsed with a moan, mortally wounded.

'Alarmed by the shouts of Clodoche, who had heard the detonation from outside on the steps, the murderer moved reflexively towards the cellar, which is where his wife found him when she arrived in the hall.

'And so, when Thérèse found her husband at the cellar door, it was not because he had just emerged from there, but because he had not had time to go down. Having only arrived at the top step, he turned to Mme. Chapon, who was coming towards him.

'And that, monsieur le juge, is the hypothesis which explains the crime in *the forbidden house.*'

'All that is unassailable logic,' declared M. Launay after a silence. 'I am happy to hear you support a theory which, incidentally, has been mine all along.'

Tom Morrow smiled at the audacious claim, but did not contradict the magistrate.

The deputy prosecutor mumbled a vague agreement. He was mentally composing his sensational closing speech for the forthcoming Arras Assizes.

Me. Chaumel murmured, in an almost indistinct voice, almost begging to be forgiven his temerity:

'If I may be permitted a simple objection?'

'I'm all ears,' replied the private detective.

'The murder weapon....'

'I thought you might ask that. Here's what I think. Charles Chapon, having discovered the entrance to the underground passage hidden behind the wine rack, and having subsequently guessed that Bénard was the author of the letters, stole his revolver. In so doing, he could divert suspicion to the guard in the event that he was found to have typed the letters.'

'What about the fingerprints found on the butt?'

'Chapon simply wore a glove, or wrapped a handkerchief around the butt.'

The defence lawyer appeared unconvinced:

'Excuse me, monsieur,' he persisted, 'but the fingerprints found on the revolver....'

'Were those of Bénard and Clodoche,' said Tom Morrow firmly, 'the owner of the weapon, and the individual who found it in the fountain after the butler had deliberately thrown in in there.'

'Obviously,' added the magistrate, as if he himself had been the author of the masterful presentation Tom Morrow had just given.

'You can see,' added the private detective, 'that the scoundrel had calculated everything down to the last minute, including the *hesitation* he showed in the presence of the other servants at the moment he made his visit to the cellar, so that, if things turned out badly, he *could claim that he had recognised Bénard but, under the threat of being shot, he had allowed him to escape through the underground passage.'*

M. Launay lit another filthy cigar and added complacently:

'He only forgot one thing, and that was that *we could prove that the concealed door had not been opened on the night of the crime.'*

'True enough. Otherwise, a cleverly conceived plan by the murderer!' concluded Tom Morrow. 'And so you can see that there's nothing inexplicable about the so-called mystery of the forbidden house.'

'We are in agreement,' replied the magistrate in a cloud of acrid smoke. 'I shall immediately release Bénard provisionally. He will only be charged with menaces, for which he will receive several months. As for Charles Chapon, even if he continues to deny his guilt, he will be arraigned before the Assizes where he will be tried by a jury for his abominable act.'

M. Launay rubbed his hands in satisfaction.

'This shows,' he said with a superior air, 'that Justice possesses the means to solve the most obscure puzzles and foil the plans of its most cunning enemies.'

'Particularly,' replied Tom Morrow with a straight face, 'when the investigation is led by a capable and perspicacious magistrate like yourself, monsieur le juge, who is not distracted by secondary matters, who proceeds methodically, and who know how to think and reason.'

'My word!' murmured M. Launay, swelling with pride. 'If you put it like that, who am I to disagree?'

VI

Radio-Paris had announced an operatic selection earlier, with choir and orchestra. Mlle. Adélaïde Balutin was normally very fond of lyrical baritones, but that evening the transmitter was silent.

The Balutin cousins were too anxious to listen to radio broadcasts.

It was the evening before the trial which was due to take place in the Arras Assizes.

The evening newspapers were strewn over the table where pieces of orange peel still lingered.

The brother and sister were arguing bitterly:

'Say what you want,' screeched the old maid, 'we've been well and truly cheated by that policeman.'

'Yet, without him, the investigation would still be making no headway! Didn't he discover the door to the underground passage and showed how the murderer used it to escape?'

'A great discovery indeed!'

'What do you mean, a great discovery? When Tom Morrow proved that the low door couldn't have been opened on the night of the murder, and that the murderer couldn't have gone out through the front door, it became clear that, after killing Verdinage, he must have stayed in the manor.'

'And then what?'

'Well, that showed clearly that it was the butler that did it. He was the main beneficiary, and if they find him guilty, he can't inherit. The bulk of the nouveau riche's fortune—which we almost lost—will come to us.'

'It's only fair! But you seem to forget that ten percent will go to Tom Morrow.'

'I repeat, without him....'

'Without him! Without him the entire gang of servants would have been charged, and we would have had, not just the Chapons' share, but all the others.'

'Obviously. But that damned policeman threatened to talk during the trial. He's very clever. Who knows what he would have said?'

159

'We should have guessed he would accuse the butler and we wouldn't have had to pay him.'

'What's done is done! Besides, who knows whether they would all have been acquitted or not? You have to admit that, before he got involved, there were several conflicting hypotheses, and the defence lawyers would have exploited the differences to plant doubt in the minds of the jury.'

This last argument impressed Adélaïde enough to halt the flood of recriminations for a moment, but she was soon back, aggressive and hateful as ever:

'As strong as your policeman is, he only made secondary discoveries. The magistrate charged Charles Chapon right at the start of his investigation... All Tom Morrow did was to show that the murderer acted alone, without an accomplice.'

'True enough.'

'Well, you imbecile, that was what should have been avoided at all costs! ... Charles will be found guilty, but Thérèse is innocent and will get to keep her share, and so will the other bumpkins. All we'll get is Charles's share, less ten percent.'

'That's better than nothing.'

'You're a failure, always have been and always will be! You're happy with what you're given and never try to rise out of your mediocrity!'

'But, Adélaïde, I never did anything without consulting you... After Tom Morrow showed us that the investigators were wrong, you were in complete agreement to pay him the commission he demanded. So?'

'So? You're an accountant. You should have seen that we were making a terrible deal. I'm convinced that the magistrate would have found a result more favourable to our interests!'

'You should have told me these excellent reasons earlier.'

'I would have done, if you hadn't panicked. But I'm going to wait for the verdict, and when Charles Chapon is convicted, I'm going to find a way to avoid paying a penny to your crooked policeman!'

'I'll be curious to find out how.'

'As clever as he is, I'll find a way, as long as my name is Adélaïde.'

'You're forgetting that there's a contract, signed, sealed and delivered.'

160

He fetched it and read it out.

Adélaïde screeched:

'It's theft! You should be ashamed.'

The accountant shrugged his shoulders and retired to his bedroom. During the night, he could hear the creaking of the bed in his sister's adjacent room, as she tossed and turned. He could hear clearly what she was saying:

'Villain!... Robber!... Bandit!...' for Tom Morrow.

'Idiot!... Dupe!... Cretin...!' for him.

That same evening, a scene of a different kind was occurring in Marchenoire Manor.

Adhémar Dupont-Lesguyères, installed in his master's armchair, had called a meeting of the manor's staff. Two were missing: Bénard, arrested for having written the anonymous letters, and Charles Chapon, due to be tried for murder the following day.

The young secretary held forth smugly at the servants, ranged in a semi-circle around him:

'I called you together to remind you to comport yourselves with dignity at the Assizes tomorrow. I'm speaking on behalf of the late Napoléon Verdinage, and I insist that your attitude be irreproachable.'

Turning to the chauffeur, he added:

'Edmond, there will be no need for the limousine. The magistrate has been kind enough to take me in his own car... I hold you accountable for buying tickets for everyone and making sure they don't miss the train tomorrow morning. As for Clodoche, make sure he washes himself and, if need be, lend him an old suit.'

Noticing that the housemaid-nanny was crying silently, he added:

'Courage, my poor Thérèse.'

The poor woman emitted a plaintive cry and began to sob desperately.

'I know how hard it is for you,' said the secretary sympathetically, 'but Justice must take its course. It's a painful necessity that no one can escape.... Besides, given the def... your husband's record, his lawyer may be able to persuade the court that there were extenuating circumstances.'

161

Thérèse was having none of it. She shook her head to indicate that she expected nothing less than a pitiless conviction. Sadly, she repeated:

'Charles!... My poor Charles!'

No one paid attention to Gustave Colinet, standing slightly apart from the other servants. Following his own random thoughts, he appeared to be daydreaming, when suddenly a flash of inspiration caused the corners of his mouth to turn up in a furtive smile.

VII

The courtroom of the Arras Assizes was full to bursting with an elegant and tumultuous crowd.

The last act of the drama of *the forbidden house* was about to play out under the vaulted ceiling of the ancient Palais des Etats d'Artois.

From the beginning to the end of the preliminary investigation, Charles Chapon had denied the charges.

The butler, who had a few supporters, had mostly detractors, who did not refrain from discussing their opinion with their neighbour.

Adding to the attraction of the mystery hanging over the proceedings was the presence of Me. Salva-Tognini, the shining star of the Paris Bar, whom the civil party, the Balutins, had retained to defend its interests.

In the centre of the room, in the exhibit showcase, lay Jacques Bénard's regulation revolver.

M. Launay entered by a hidden door and took a seat behind the tribunal. A murmur circulated in the crowd. People pointed to the man the press had been eulogising for the last month. The magistrate had come to watch his triumph.

He responded with a patronizing gesture to the deferential salutes of some of the citizens.

Suddenly he ducked his head and pretended to be absorbed in reading a brief: he had just noticed Tom Morrow amongst the public, where his presence attracted some curiosity.

The usher announced in a rasping voice:

'Messieurs, la Cour.'

The President of the Assizes placed his hat in front of him, spoke to his assistants, and opened a thick dossier. He was a solemn and formidable judge whose reputation struck fear into malefactors.

He knew how to keep the proceedings moving briskly and bring easy-going jurors to heel.

Me. Malicorne took the state prosecutor's seat, not without affectation, pleased to be the centre of attention.

The attention of the spectators was soon focused on Me. Salva-

Tognini. They almost applauded the entrance of the bearded colossus with the thundering voice, who sat down proudly on the civil party's bench, dominating the room with his imperious regard.

The self-effacing and shy Me. Chaumel looked anxiously at his colleague, against whom he was supposed to argue eloquently. The trenchant voice of the president caused him to jump.

'Bring in the accused!'

A door creaked open and the accused appeared.

Charles Chapon, dazzled by the bright light and the noise, recoiled reflexively.

The journalists waited attentively, pen in hand.

The butler took his place beside two hefty gendarmes.

He already looked overwhelmed by fate. All his energy had been spent in the magistrate's chambers. Now, despair—and perhaps remorse—rendered him indifferent as to his fate.

The president ordered the courtroom to be quiet and read out the standard questions:

'Your name?'

'Chapon.'

'Your first names?'

'Charles, Marie, Célestin.'

'Your profession?'

'Butler, in the service of Monsieur Verdinage for twelve years.'

'Clerk, read the indictment.'

The document gathered together all of Tom Morrow's arguments. It destroyed the accused with its logic and concision.

Even the butler's most fervent supporters had to admit the case against him seemed conclusive. It remained to be seen whether his defence would successfully argue extenuating circumstances.

When the reading was complete, the president asked:

'Charles Chapon, have you anything to say?'

'I'm innocent! I'm innocent!' muttered the butler.

Indignant protests could be heard coming from several parts of the courtroom.

'What an actor!'

The president was obliged to intervene:

'If these outbursts continue, I shall be obliged to have the courtroom cleared.'

Silence followed, as if by magic.

The president ordered the accused to present facts to countermand those which proved his obvious guilt.

But Charles merely repeated wearily:

'I'm innocent! I'm innocent!'

Me. Salva-Tognini got to his feet, his robes flapping, and proclaimed:

'All the accused does is deny. He denies everything, including the evidence. The members of the jury will understand this overly simple means of defence.'

'Why are we being criticised?' retorted Me. Chaumel. 'For being innocent and proclaiming it? Should we confess to a crime, of which we are innocent, just to please our illustrious colleague?'

'We are asking you to respond to the precise accusations being lodged against you,' barked the deputy.

The president abruptly curtailed the verbal duel between the lawyers.

'The matter is closed,' he announced. 'Usher, bring in the first witness.'

Thérèse crossed the courtroom. A thick veil half covered her face ravaged by tears.

Gripping the bar, she defended her husband vigorously.

Incapable of dishonesty, the housemaid-nanny would not admit that Charles was a scoundrel, despite all the evidence.

'He's a drunk, a ne'er-do-well, but not a murderer,' she maintained.

She had to admit, when pressed by Me. Malicorne, that the butler had left the conjugal bedroom during the night of October 28 and that she had found him in the cellar doorway when she arrived in the hall, shortly after the shot was fired.

'He had gone down there to drink,' she added.

Me. Salva-Tognini, robes flapping, thundered:

'It's not a question of putting forward a hypothesis, but of giving evidence. Can you, under oath, *assert that the accused was not in the hall at the time of the murder?*'

Thérèse remained silent.

Me. Salva-Tognini bowed:

'Thank you, madame.'

Edmond, Jeanne, Gustave, Adhémar, and Clodoche appeared in

turn to describe their movements during the tragic night.

Bénard, released from prison, caused a sensation.

Me. Chaumel pointed a threatening finger at him:

'I don't know what credit the state prosecutor and the civil party attach to the words of this witness, who was found guilty of lying during the preliminary investigation,' declared the young lawyer, 'and I don't know for what reason two cases that are intimately entwined have been separated. Your place, Bénard, is not on the witness stand, but in the dock, alongside the person I am charged with defending.'

'He's insulting the witness,' howled Me. Salva-Tognini.

The guard withdrew.

Lieutenant Taupinois, dressed in a tight-fitting uniform, recited his report, which he had learnt by heart.

M. Duran, weapons expert, certified, in obscure technical terms, that the revolver found in the fountain by Clodoche was incontestably the murder weapon.

Docteur Pierre, medical examiner, described the position of the body and the wound caused by the bullet.

'My conclusion,' he said, 'is that the murderer was approximately five metres from Verdinage when he fired. He was therefore standing roughly at the entrance of the library.'

There were loud murmurs from those present as Me. Salva-Tognini stood up.

Arms spread wide, he seemed to sweep away the obstinate denials of the accused.

His powerful voice resonated throughout the courtroom.

'There is an attempt to create an atmosphere of mystery about this case,' he boomed. 'Members of the jury, I invite you to disregard the phantasmagorical nonsense about *a forbidden house*, and concentrate on the realities of the case.

'Let us call things by their real name. You are being asked to decide a criminal case, nothing more. There is a murderer, one who committed one of the most vile acts possible—one who murders his own benefactor!

'A villainous crime, members of the jury. Chapon cynically murdered the man to whom he owed everything, in order to save his inheritance, an inheritance that he was in danger of losing.

'One indisputable fact dominates the argument: Verdinage's

murderer could not have left the manor after perpetrating his vile deed... He must therefore be *amongst the number of servants in residence there... amongst the servants who were inside the residence when the shot was fired.* Of all such servants, *only one* could logically have killed Verdinage, and *only one* had a motive to do so... And there he is!... Charles Chapon!

'Members of the jury, you must be merciless. In the name of the victim, and in the name of a family in mourning, I demand a just and necessary punishment.

'I demand the full application of the law in all its rigour!'

Thérèse, seated in the courtroom, gave a heart-rending cry and fainted. She was carried out.

Then it was the turn of the state prosecutor.

Me. Malicorne rose slowly, cleared his throat, stroked his beard, which spread out over his red robe, and began:

'Charles Chapon killed!'

'He was seen by his wife, in the hall, a few moments after the shot was fired. The time taken for Thérèse Capon to recover and reach the hall was amply sufficient for the murderer to reach the cellar door, where Mme. Chapon saw her husband. Chapon was alone in the hall at the time.

'The valet Gustave Colinet, the chauffeur Edmond Tasseau, and the cook Jeanne Tasseau were upstairs... Not to mention the servants outside, and consequently above suspicion, namely: the guard Jacques Bénard and his assistant Clodoche... nor the secretary Adhémar Dupont-Lesguyères, a long way away... *No one other than Chapon could have killed Verdinage....*'

He concluded:

'For society's sake, members of the jury, be resolute... I demand the death penalty.'

The accused shrank even further.

'Let the defence be heard!' said the president.

Me. Chauvet stood up. A few papers fell to the floor. In the dreadful, agonising silence he began:

'Messieurs de la Cour, Messieurs les Jurés,

'I could, faced with the facts presented so eloquently, plead diminished responsibility, due to the effects of intemperate consumption by the old man seated in the dock.

167

'But, in so doing, I would not have a clear conscience about doing my duty.

'A moment ago, Me. Salva-Tognini accused me of creating a fantasmagorical atmosphere.

'Nevertheless, messieurs les jurés, there is a mystery hanging over this case. The examining magistrate believed it possible to separate the threatening letters from the criminal affair.

'I, on the other hand, assert that there is an obvious connection between those letters and Verdinage's murder.

'Verdinage, messieurs les jurés, was killed on the night following the delivery of the death warrant, just as his predecessor, Desrousseaux, was killed two years earlier.

'In the two cases, the same order: leave, or face the same violent end—except that Desrousseaux was killed with a rifle and Verdinage with a revolver.

'Other owners received the same threats, but prudently left, which surely saved their lives.

'All the letters were typed on the same machine, which was found in the guardhouse. Despite his protests, Jacques Bénard was found guilty of having sent the letters and convicted.

'Both the typewriter and the revolver belonged to the same individual.

'And, let us not forget, messieurs les jurés, Verdinage did not like the guard, who, on several occasions tried to persuade him to leave Marchenoire Manor.

'Need I remind you that Bénard was also employed by Desrousseaux, who was also mysteriously murdered?

'"Coincidence," says the prosecution.

'A curious coincidence indeed, to be sure.

'Messieurs les jurés, like it or not, there is a mystery, the mystery of *the forbidden house*. To demonstrate just how mysterious, the examining magistrate's suspicions fell on no less than four other people before settling on Charles Chapon, and Charles Chapon alone!

'Messieurs les jurés, it seems obvious that Verdinage's murderer could not have left the manor after committing his crime. It also seems obvious that he could not have hidden inside and evaded the successive searches of the servants and the police.

'I am not disputing *that Charles Chapon was present in the hall, if*

168

not during the crime, at least within a few seconds of it.

'Study the plan of Marchenoire Manor, messieurs les jurés, as I have over many sleepless nights.

'Perhaps you will prove to be more perspicacious than I, and will find an explanation for the mystery of *the forbidden house*, an explanation that will absolve my client?

'Messieurs les jurés, I will close by saying that the many discussions with Charles Chapon over many long weeks have convinced me of one thing: Charles Chapon is not guilty!'

Me. Chaumel wiped his pale brow, which was covered in perspiration.

The young lawyer had succeeded in creating an atmosphere of mystery, which had visibly impressed several of the jurors, but others had realised that, unable to refute the facts put forward by the prosecution, he had cleverly tried to cast doubt into the consciences of those who would decide his client's fate.

The president asked the butler:

'Is there anything the accused wishes to add in his defence?'

Charles Chapon moaned in a broken voice:

'It wasn't me! It wasn't me!'

This last denial received a widespread murmur of disapproval. Charles Chapon's obstinacy overcame the momentary benefit of his counsel's skilful defence. The jurors were now decided that the butler deserved the ultimate punishment.

Me. Chaumel understood and gave a gesture of despair.

The jurors stood up, ready to retire to their chamber for deliberations.

VIII

Just as the jury was about to retire, Me. Chaumel got to his feet, still very pale.

'I have just been handed a card from witness Colinet, who asks to be heard,' he said. 'He apparently has some important revelations to make. In the name of truth, I beg la Cour to let him be heard.'

The president, clearly annoyed by the late intervention disturbing the smooth functioning of the hearings, nevertheless grumbled:

'By virtue of the discretionary power vested in me, I authorise the witness Gustave Colinet to complete his testimony.'

The valet crossed the courtroom, embarrassed to be the focal point of the hearings.

The president ordered him in an unfriendly tone:

'Turn to face Messieurs les jurés and give your testimony.'

Gustave Colinet gathered his thoughts for a moment and declared:

'Monsieur Charles is not guilty, and I am here to reveal the name of M. Napoléon Verdinage's true murderer.'

A murmur rippled through the courtroom.

Me. Salva-Tognini got to his feet and thundered:

'La partie civile will not tolerate such manoeuvres! If the witness really has such serious assertions, why is he making them at this late hour, when arguments have been concluded? These are just dramatics, explicable but not excusable by the enthusiasm and youth of the counsel for the defence.'

Me. Chaumel retorted:

'I demand that my learned colleague retract his words immediately.'

Me. Malicorne decided to enter the war of words:

'It's obvious that—.'

The president cut him off peremptorily:

'The incident is closed.'

He continued, addressing Colinet:

'La Cour is surprised by your late intervention. Why did you not bring the matter up during your earlier testimony?'

Gustave Colinet did not appear to be concerned by the president's aggressive attitude. He replied simply:

'I only received the *proof* I need a few minutes ago.'

'Even without such *proof*, you must have harboured suspicions for a long time. Why did you not convey them to the juge d'instruction?'

'*I could not*, monsieur le president.'

'What prevented you?'

'*The circumstances*, monsieur le president.'

'Please turn to le jury and explain.'

Gustave Colinet coughed, then, in a voice devoid of all emotion, began:

'Messieurs les jurés, I am neither a policeman nor a prosecutor and do not pretend to be either.

'Nevertheless, I did believe that I was allowed to think about the odious crime that you have been called upon to pass judgment.

'Long before my master was murdered, and as soon as I learnt about a mysterious writer sending threatening letters to successive owners of Marchenoire Manor, I tried to find a reason why anyone would act in such a way and create the mystery of *the forbidden house.*

'I haven't forgotten—and neither should you, messieurs les jurés — the fraud committed by the banker Goldenberg. During the investigation into that fraud, one *detail* struck me.

'*The twenty million francs he stole were never recovered*, despite no stone being left unturned in the search.

'The banker, who lived frugally, could not possibly have spent it all himself, and the stolen money was not used to renovate Marchenoire Manor.

'It was also determined that no capital funds had been transferred to any country in South America, the banker's destination when he was arrested.

'One question dominated the headlines of the day:

'"*Where did the twenty million francs go?*"

'They must obviously have been hidden in a safe, secure spot. It occurred to me that such a spot may lie within the boundaries of Marchenoire Manor, his last residence.

'Goldenberg died shortly after going to prison and his wife poisoned herself in despair.

'Is it not likely that, just before his death, the banker revealed the approximate location of the loot to a fellow comrade in chains?

'That would explain *why someone would show such a particularly stubborn interest in the forbidden house.*

'It would also explain why the guardian of the secret did not possess the means necessary to purchase the manor, or he would have done so and continued his search in peace and quiet.

'In any case, the convict, released or fugitive, would be very poor and reluctant to share his secret with anyone else.

'Once the hypothesis occurred to me, I set about verifying it.

'It just so happens that my elder brother, Isadore Colinet, has worked for ten years in the service of M. le directeur de la Sûreté generale, where he has access to inmate information.

'I wrote to him to ask for a list of convicts released between the date of Goldenberg's arrest and the first threatening letter received by Desrousseaux. No convict escaped during that period.

'The description of one of those freed drew my attention. I asked for more details about convict No. 223.

'Here is a letter, members of the jury, which was delivered to Marchenoire Manor in my absence, and which has just been given to me here, in accordance with my instructions.

'The letter, which I have been waiting for impatiently, and which I would have liked to receive at the beginning of these hearings, informs me that convict No. 223 was working in the infirmary in the last weeks of his sentence. He was there when Goldenberg died.

'Convict No. 223 was released the following day and disappeared shortly thereafter.

'Less than six months later, M. Desrousseaux was murdered in the park of *the forbidden house.*

'It is probable that the banker did not have the time to describe the precise location of the buried loot, or it would have been dug up straight away, and all the mysterious events which culminated in the death of M. Verdinage would never have occurred.

'As I speak, the treasure has still not been found.

'Since his return from the penal colony, convict No. 223 has been searching for it relentlessly. This sinister individual quickly tumbled to the trick the guard Bénard was playing, sending letters to successive owners to frighten them off.

'He benefitted from Bénard's idea in the sense that he blamed a fictitious person for his crimes: he didn't hesitate to kill M. Desrousseaux and, later, M. Verdinage, who both refused to leave *the forbidden house.'*

'*I will tell you the identity of convict No. 223 in a moment.*

'You now understand, messieurs les jurés, why I did not have the right to reveal the results of my research until I could provide *proof* of Charles Chapon's innocence.

'*That proof* was under my nose on the night of the crime, when the servants were all assembled in the hall, but, *distracted by another event, just like everyone else*, I failed to see the truth.

'And yet it was so simple!....'

Gustave paused for a moment.

Me. Chaumel was exultant. Without knowing how the witness was going to explain the crime, which only seemed explicable by admitting the guilt of his client, he felt confident that Gustave Colinet's implacable logic would finally establish his client's innocence.

The deputy objected angrily:

'Whilst I compliment the witness for his perspicacity, there is nevertheless an important fact, upon which I must insist. It has been established that Charles Chapon was not in his room at the time of the crime. It has rightly been supposed that, taking advantage of his wife being asleep, he left silently and went down to the park gate where, face covered, he presented himself to Clodoche, who was waiting there for the mysterious visitor announced in the third threatening letter.'

Gustave turned to the jurors to answer:

'Messieurs les jurés, may I remind you that, during the night of October 28 to 29, it rained very heavily.

'If M. Charles had indeed gone down to the gate and back, in Clodoche's company, he would have been soaked to the skin!

'I can confirm—and Thérèse Chapon, Edmond and Jeanne Tasseau can confirm as well—that Charles Chapon was not wet when, one by one, we arrived in the hall.

'By contrast, Jacques Bénard and M. Dupont-Lesguyères, who came in later, were soaked from head to foot.

'On the night of the crime, it was impossible to be outside for more

174

than five minutes without getting drenched. Yet M. Charles, I repeat, had not a single drop of water on his clothes.

'The strange visitor was therefore not the butler.

'That detail, obvious when one thinks about it, escaped my attention because, like everyone else, I was baffled by the sudden disappearance of the murderer.

'There can be no doubt about it. The guard Bénard saw Clodoche arrive with someone whose features were obscured by his coat and by the darkness. I myself saw Clodoche and the visitor arrive.

'Mme. Thérèse heard the footsteps on the gravel. Blessed with exceptional hearing, she also detected the scraping of shoes on the steps, the sound of the cripple's crutch on the stone, and the metallic click of the lantern being placed in front of the door.

'Those last two details prove that Clodoche went up the steps behind the visitor, who did indeed go into the hallway.

'Because other witnesses have testified that, once inside the manor, the murderer could not have got out, it would be tempting to conclude, as M. Tom Morrow, private detective, has done, that the murderer was in the hall with M. Verdinage's servants.

'Let us nevertheless see, messieurs les jurés, whether there is not another solution. To do that, we must proceed by elimination, excluding no one.

'Clodoche, who only came in after the shot was fired, in other words, after M. Charles opened the door, seems to be ruled out.

'I saw, with my own eyes, the chauffeur Edmond go down the stairs after the detonation was heard.

'I myself—you see that I also include myself!—went down after him.

'Jeanne Tasseau arrived after me.

'Jacques Bénard arrived even later.

'M. Dupont-Lesguyères was absent.

'Mme. Thérèse and M. Charles were the first ones into the hall. They do not deny it and their testimony is rigorously exact. If they had left the manor they would have been soaked.

'They were both perfectly dry.

'That observation, which exonerates them, exonerates all the servants who slept in Marchenoire Manor on the night of the crime.'

'At the moment we were all gathered before the corpse of M.

175

Verdinage, there were seven of us, to wit: M. Charles and Mme. Thérèse, Edmond and Jeanne Tasseau, Jacques Bénard, Clodoche and myself.

'There were seven of us, and there should have been eight, because the visitor introduced by Clodoche could not have been one of us seven.

'There was no getting away from it. The eighth person had to be found before the problem could be considered solved.

'It was only today, when I received my brother's letter, that I finally found the eighth person.'

IX

The third juror asked a question:
'How is it that *the eighth person* was only seen by the witness?'
Gustave Colinet replied:
'I don't believe I said that I was the only one to have seen the eighth person. *We all saw him.*'
Me. Salva-Tognini rose indignantly, robes flapping:
'*You have just declared that the mysterious visitor introduced by Clodoche was not amongst those gathered with you in the hall.*'
'*That is correct.*'
'And yet Clodoche did indeed introduce someone into the manor?'
'*That is undeniable.*'
'Did that eighth person leave?'
'*No!*'
'Could he not have hidden somewhere on the premises?'
'*That would have been impossible.*'
'When you were all assembled in the hall, was he there?'
'No!'
'Where was he at that moment?'
'*In the library.*'
The president intervened:
'But there was only Verdinage's corpse in the library.'
Gustave Colinet replied, without raising his voice:
'*He was the eighth person.*'
M. Malicorne got to his feet, arms raised to the heavens:
'The witness seems to be insinuating that the victim killed himself. The reports of the medical examiner and the weapons expert are clear. Verdinage was killed by a bullet fired from a distance of approximately five metres, and the murder weapon was found in the fountain. Verdinage was murdered.
'Furthermore, Lieutenant Taupinois found a Browning of a different calibre in the victim's pocket with a full magazine.'
'Did I claim anything different?' retorted Gustave.
'I thought that...,' stammered the deputy, flustered by the reply.

177

Me. Chaumel said nervously:

'I ask the witness to explain.'

The valet bowed formally:

'With your permission, I shall do so shortly.'

He continued his explanation:

'We know, from the pencil line drawn across the bottom of the third letter, that M. Verdinage was still waiting for his mysterious visitor at quarter past twelve.

'M. Verdinage, whom we all saw go up to his bedroom at ten o'clock, went back downstairs surreptitiously at midnight and shut himself in the library.

'Fifteen minutes later, seeing no one coming, he wrote the phrase we know at the foot of the page:

'*"A quarter past twelve... Nothing."*

'The visitor was making him wait.

'Not only did the visitor make him wait, *he never turned up at the park gate where Clodoche himself was waiting.*

'At around half past twelve, no longer prepared to wait—and perhaps anxious that the cripple might have been attacked or even killed by the visitor—the frustrated owner of *the forbidden house* put on a hat and a raincoat that had been hanging behind the front door since the inclement weather had begun. Still careful to avoid waking anyone, M. Verdinage went out without making the slightest noise.

'At the park gate he found Clodoche who, following orders, was waiting there with his lantern covered for the visitor who was supposed to come.

'Not seeing signs of anyone on the road from Compiègne, M. Verdinage decided to go back, and Clodoche accompanied him as far as the top of the steps.

'M. Verdinage took off the hat and raincoat and hung them behind the door and gave vent to his feelings by declaring loudly the words overheard by Mme. Thérèse:

'*"No! I won't leave!"*

'Suddenly, turning round, he found himself *face to face with convict No. 223!*'

The president pointed to Colinet impatiently and said:

'I order you to tell la Cour and Messieurs les jurés the identity of convict No. 223.'

178

Gustave Colinet pulled a paper out of his pocket.

'Will la Cour allow me to read out the brief notes communicated to me about the said convict?'

The president conferred with his associates and replied:

'Even though it is very irregular, I shall allow it.'

The valet read out the notes:

'Joseph Bigot, 41 years of age, was sentenced to five years of hard labour for fraud and embezzlement. His sentence was reduced for good behaviour and he was allowed to work as a nurse.

'Height: 1 m. 65.

'Hair colour: red.

'During his incarceration, he was the victim of an accident which caused a complex fracture of the pelvis.

'Nevertheless, he left the penal colony upon his release and has not been heard from for two years. He is believed to be in France.

'Distinguishing characteristic: a pronounced limp.'

The president wrote a few words on a card and passed it to the deputy. Malicorne nodded and handed the card to the usher.

The latter looked surprised and left by a side door, returning almost immediately to his seat.

Me. Chaumel exclaimed:

'But isn't the description the witness has just given us that of....'

'... Clodoche?' Me. Salva-Tognini finished the sentence.

Gustave Colinet nodded in agreement.

'Exactly.

'Joseph Bigot, ex-convict No. 223, is Clodoche.

'It is he who followed M. Verdinage into the hall.

'You can imagine the latter's horror when he saw the scoundrel pointing a revolver at him.

'Clodoche fired. M. Verdinage fell to the floor, uttering a heart-rending cry.

'The criminal only had to take two steps back in order to find himself on the steps next to the lantern.

'He slammed the front door and banged on it with his crutch whilst shouting at the top of his voice.

'Bénard couldn't see the steps from his hiding-place. He had seen Clodoche arrive, escorting M. Verdinage (whom he did not recognise in the darkness), but he was unaware that the cripple had entered the

179

manor, thinking that he had remained outside next to the lantern.

'I made a similar error when I heard Clodoche banging on the door from the outside. It never occurred to me that he could have gone in and out *whilst I went from my window to the door and back.*

'It was only when I received the description of convict No. 223 a short while ago that I was able to reconstruct the crime.

The president stood up solemnly and said to the witness:

'On behalf of la Cour, allow me to congratulate you publicly. You have acted, Monsieur Gustave Colinet, like a detective of the first calibre. I have sent for Joseph Bigot, otherwise known as Clodoche, to return to Court to hear the outcome of this trial.'

Me. Malicorne added his voice:

'Le Ministère publique joins in the praise for the witness.'

Me. Chaumel exclaimed emotionally:

'Upon my word, the innocent party that you have saved thanks you!'

Charles Chapon was unable to say anything. Overcome by emotion, he cried silently.

The lawyer continued:

'Your version, Monsieur Gustave Colinet, explains everything. There are no loose ends.

'The fingerprints found on the murder weapon are those of Bénard, the owner, and Clodoche, who used it. The latter's fingerprints are explained by the fact that he "found" the weapon where he had thrown it: in the fountain.

'After he left the penal colony, and having learnt of the existence of the treasure, Clodoche hung around Marchenoire and discovered that Desrousseaux occupied the property. He also heard about the three threatening letters which had had no effect on the occupant.

'One night, ex-convict No. 223 put an end to the troublemaker's days by shooting him with a rifle.

'Shortly thereafter, the miscreant made Bénard's acquaintance, wormed his way into the latter's good books, and was given a job on the estate.

'Other threatening letters chased away later owners.

'Whilst Bénard, an incorrigible poacher, roamed the woods at night, Clodoche, left alone, searched tirelessly for the hidden treasure.

'How could anyone suspect the unfortunate cripple who had free rein of the premises?

'On the night of the crime, this odious individual assumed, correctly, that Verdinage would start to get worried when no one turned up at the time given in the third letter. He guessed that his master would go down to the park gate. Waiting for an opportune moment to kill him, he walked back up with his master under the pretext of lighting his path.

'He decided to act when he found himself in the hall.

'Maybe Verdinage invited him inside for a hot drink, to thank him for standing out in the rain.'

Me. Chaumel stopped at that point.

Shouts rang out in the courtroom

The cripple came in, pushed by a gendarme.

'What?... What?... What does anyone want with poor Clodoche?'

'I'm placing you under arrest,' retorted the president.

'Clodoche doesn't know... Clodoche asks....'

'Bigot, Joseph, ex-convict No. 223, I'm charging you with the murder of Napoléon Verdinage!'

Clodoche looked up in surprise.

The expression on his face suddenly changed, as if a mask had slipped.

A cruel smile replaced the idiotic leer.

Clodoche appeared as his true self: Joseph Bigot, ex-convict:

'It's a fair catch. I'm not going to complain. Just go gently on me.'

He put his hands out to be cuffed and was led out to the prison van.

And so ended the first adventure of Gustave Colinet, amateur detective.

THE END

APPENDIX I: THE FRENCH JUDICIAL SYSTEM

In the British and American systems, the police and prosecution gather information likely to convict the suspect. The defence gathers information likely to acquit the defendant. Arguments between the two, and the examination of witnesses, are conducted in open court, and refereed by a judge. The winner is decided, in most important cases, by a jury of ordinary citizens.

In the French system, also adopted in many other continental countries, all criminal cases are investigated by an examining magistrate (Juge d'instruction) who is appointed and given his brief by the public prosecutor (Le Parquet) . He or she is independent of the government and the prosecution service, and works with the police. Much of the evaluation of the evidence goes on, in secret, during the investigation: confrontations between witnesses; recreations of the crime, etc.) The final report of the examining magistrate is supposed to contain all the evidence favourable to both defence and prosecution.

The investigations are frequently long—two years in straightforward cases is normal—but trials are mostly short. Witnesses are called and the evidence is rehearsed in court, but lengthy cross-examination in the British/American manner is rare. The case is presented by the public prosecutor, who goes by the title of Le Parquet (wooden floor) because he or she has to stand on the floor to argue the case before Le Tribunal of three judges (a president and two associates) seated above them. The word Assizes comes from the French for seated (assises). The nine members of the jury are selected at random by lottery.

A civil party who believes the actions of the accused have caused financial loss may have his case enjoined with that of the public, and his attorney prosecute in tandem.

In France, as in Britain, the defendant is theoretically innocent until proven guilty but, in practice, there is a strong presumption of guilt if an examining magistrate, having weighed the evidence, recommends prosecution. Not to mention the fact that the prosecution and police are frequently present when witnesses are questioned.

There is no right of habeas corpus in France. Investigating magistrates have a right (within limits) to imprison suspects for lengthy periods without trial, which can be a handy way of extracting evidence. Suspects can admit or deny their guilt, but their plea makes little difference to the nature of the investigation and trial. French jails are full of people who have not been charged.

Much of the leg-work is done by the police (in towns) or gendarmerie (in rural areas). Criminal matters are pursued by the judicial police (Police Judiciaire), which includes the flying squad (Brigade Mobile), often in conflict with the gendarmerie. Public order, including traffic control, is performed by the administrative police (Police Administrative).

Paris, needless to say, has its own police prefecture (Préfecture de police de Paris), originally located at the legendary Quai des Orfèvres, the first home of the equally legendary Sûreté, the inspiration for the (even more legendary) Scotland Yard.

The two ranks of the Police Judiciaire mentioned in many stories are commissaire (equivalent to superintendent) and brigadier (equivalent to sergeant).

As a tangentially-related piece of trivia, the nickname for arsenic in French is "poudre de succession"—inheritance powder.

APPENDIX II: THE FRENCH GOLDEN AGE

To my knowledge, there is no accepted definition of a French locked room Golden Age, but—despite the isolated activities of Gaston Leroux in 1907-08; Boileau-Narcejac as a team in the 1950s; Martin Méroy in the 1960s; and the one-man Golden Age of Paul Halter starting in the 1980s—it is hard to deny that the preponderance of authors and titles occurred between 1930 and 1948. Much of the information below comes from the excellent bibliography *1000 Chambres Closes,* by Roland Lacourbe *et al.*

1930 saw the appearance of Pierre Véry's *Le Testament de Basil Crookes* (The Testament of Basil Crookes), and 1948 was the year that Thomas Narcejac's *La Mort est du voyage* (Death on Board) won the *Grand Prix du Roman d'aventures,* France's international award for mystery fiction (He and Boileau met at Narcejac's award dinner.)

The period between those years saw three prolific authors: Maurice Leblanc, Noël Vindry and the Belgian Stanislas-André Steeman; Pierre Boileau and Thomas Narcejac writing separately; and many of what Roland Lacourbe calls "shooting stars"—authors who produced one or two books in a very short period, then disappeared from sight.

Maurice Leblanc is best known for his short stories featuring ArsèneLupin, but his gentleman thief also appears in two novels: La *Barre-y-va* (The Barre-y-va) in 1932, and *La Femme aux deux sourires* (The Woman With Two Smiles) in 1933.

Of Steeman's more than thirty novels, five contained locked room puzzles: *Six homes morts* (Six Dead Men) and *La Nuit du 12 au 13* (The Night of the 12th and 13th) in 1931; *Zéro* (Zero) in 1932; *L'Ennemi sans visage* (The Enemy Without a Face) in 1934; and *L'Infaillible Silas Lord* (The Infallible Silas Lord) in 1938.

Vindry also wrote more than thirty novels, but is best known for his ten locked room mysteries, notably *La Bête hurlante* (The Howling Beast*) and *Le Double Alibi* (The Double Alibi*) in 1934; *À travers les murailles* (Through the Walls) in 1937; *La Fuite des morts* (The Vanishing Dead) in 1933: and *La Maison qui tue* (The House That Kills*) in 1932.

Pierre Boileau wrote *La Pierre qui tremble* (The Shifting Rock) in 1934; *Le Repos de Bacchus* (The Sleeping Bacchus), which won the *Grand Prix du Roman d'aventures,* in 1938; his masterpiece *Six Crimes Sans Assassin* (literally Six Crimes Without a Killer) in 1935; writing as Anicot, *Un Assassin au chateau* (A Killer in the Castle) in 1944; and *L'Assassin vient les mains vides* (The Killer Comes Empty-Handed) in 1945. In addition to the aforementioned *La Mort est du voyage,* Narcejac also wrote *L'Assassin de Minuit (*The Midnight Killer*)* in 1945.

Amongst the shooting stars are, in alphabetical order:

-Gaston Boca, who wrote four novels between 1933 and 1935, of which two, *L'Ombre sur le jardin* (The Shadow Over the Garden) in1933, and *Les Invités de minuit* (The Seventh Guest*) in 1935, are regarded as early classics. The remaining two: *Les Usines de l'effroi* (The Terror Factories) in1934,and *Le Dîner de Mantes* (Dinner at Mantes) in 1935, both have weak solutions.

-Antoine Chollier who wrote *Dossier n°7* (Dossier n°7) in 1946.

-Alexis Gensoul, who wrote *L'Énigma de Tefaha* (The Riddle of Tefaha)*;* *Gribouille est mort* (Gribouille Is Dead); and—with Charles Grenier—*La Mort vient de nulle part* (Death out of Nowhere*), all in 1945, whilst a conscript in the French army.

-Michel Herbert and EugèneWyl, who together wrote *La Maison interdite* (The Forbidden House*) in 1932; and *Le Crime derrière la porte* (The Crime Behind the Door) in 1934.

-Marcel Lanteaume, whose *Orage sur la Grande Semaine* (Storm Over Festival Week) in 1944; *Trompe-l'œil* (Trompe-l'Œil) in 1946; and *La Treizième balle* (The Thirteenth Bullet*) in 1948, were all written whilst he was a prisoner-of-war in a German concentration camp.

-Roch de Santa-Maria who wrote *Pendu trop court* (Hanged Too Short) in 1937, based on a real-life impossible crime.

Several of the foregoing novels may well be candidates for future LRI publication.

*Already published by LRI